Legends of the Unseen

J. C. Brandt

Published by J. C. Brandt, 2024.

This is a work of fiction. Similarities to real people, places, or events are entirely coincidental.

LEGENDS OF THE UNSEEN

First edition. November 10, 2024.

Copyright © 2024 J. C. Brandt.

ISBN: 979-8227713902

Written by J. C. Brandt.

Table of Contents

Legends of the Unseen 1
Ethereal Pirates: Bound by Fate 26
The Forgotten Pack 75
Spheres of Confinement 99

"A Legacy of Family Secrets and Ancient Powers"

He stood there, bewildered and dazed, grappling with the sheer horror of the scene that lay before him. His eyes, still moist with tears, tried to make sense of the crimson chaos that surrounded him. Blood was splattered everywhere like an artist's twisted masterpiece, and the lifeless body of Jack lay motionless at his feet.

The gun in his hand felt heavy, and he could feel the heat emanating from it. Had he pulled the trigger? Had he ended Jack's life with his own two hands? But there were no visible signs of a gunshot on Jack's body, at least not any that he could discern. As he looked down at his own body, he realized he too was bleeding profusely from his right side. What had happened here? And where were the others? He tried to recall who he had come with. Jane, Bob, and Katy, that's right. But where were they now? The place was unfamiliar to him, and he couldn't remember how he had ended up there. Perhaps it was Jack's uncle's or aunt's retreat, but he couldn't be certain. The questions swirled in his mind, and he knew that he had to find answers. But first, he had to confront the possibility that he may have killed his friend in cold blood.

Red's hand trembled as he placed the gun on the blood-soaked floor, his mind reeling from the surreal horror that had unfolded before him. Pain seared through his body, and he winced as he attempted to rise from the pool of blood that had engulfed him.

The nagging suspicion that he had been shot gnawed at him relentlessly. Fearful of what he might find, he hesitated to inspect the wound, but he knew he had to. With a shaky hand, he lifted his shirt and peered down at his torso. Sure enough, there was a bloody hole in his flesh.

But the more pressing question was, had he done this to himself, or had he been in a scuffle with someone? And if so, why was Jack dead? Red's anguished cry echoed through the empty house, but there was no response.

Desperate to escape the gruesome scene, Red dragged himself through the house, propelled by a primal instinct to survive. Outside, he scanned the area for a vehicle he could commandeer and use to get to the hospital. But as he pondered his next move, a deep sense of dread crept over him. Would he get into trouble if he sought help? He didn't remember much after arriving at the place, except for Jack's welcoming toast. "Welcome to the country, bitches," he yelled.

Now, Red was trapped in a nightmare of blood, betrayal, and confusion, with no way out but forward. There was no vehicle outside. His phone was destroyed. Perhaps Jack still had his phone on him, Red thought. He couldn't understand why the sight of his deceased friend didn't cause him to panic, but he attributed it to a state of shock. He ventured back into the house and rifled through Jack's pockets, but there was no phone to be found. The pain in his side was unbearable and threatened to knock him unconscious. Though he attempted to apply pressure to the wound, the agony was too great to endure. Scouring the house yielded no results, and Red realized that he would need to venture elsewhere on foot. Gazing into the distance for any indication of civilization, he made his way down the long driveway and onto a gravel path. His progress was sluggish, and the pain was all-consuming. Eventually, he could go no further, and he collapsed at the roadside, half-conscious.

His stupor was broken by the sound of a vehicle pulling up beside him, and the footsteps of strangers drawing nearer. "He looks dead," a female voice observed. "It doesn't matter, mama will want to see him regardless," a man's voice responded. The strangers hefted Red into the back of their truck, he hoped that they were coming to his aid. The journey was fraught with jolts and jarring movements, and Red could barely endure the torment. He was dragged inside a building upon arrival and deposited onto a couch in the center of the room. An elderly woman approached him, but his senses were hazy, and he could barely discern her features. As she drew nearer, he glimpsed a dagger in her grasp. "I see that they failed in their task," she muttered. "Their blunder has thrust us into the hunt, but you will ensure our protection." Red's confusion mounted as she plunged the blade into his heart. His struggles were futile, and he succumbed to the injury, his spirit departing from his body as he gazed upon his lifeless form.

"You will not be departing just yet," the old woman intoned, trapping his spirit within a jar. "Prepare him," she instructed the others. They hoisted him onto a mammoth slab of stone, trussing his limbs and head. The old woman then proceeded to eviscerate him with expert precision, removing his brain after offering a prayer. She retrieved a jar of her creation and sprinkled its contents into the cavity. With swift and steady hands, she grasped the jar containing his essence and a colossal bottle, adorned with an enigmatic emblem, and poured their contents into the gaping wounds. As she meticulously sewed him back together, she beseeched the heavens above for guidance and aid. The culmination of her efforts bore fruit, as Red awoke from his slumber, yet something felt askew. His vision was altered, enabling him to see not only the elderly crone but also a youthful damsel and an aged, portly gentleman. However, his sight was not limited to mere mortals, for his gaze perceived an array of fantastical entities, some splendid while others elicited terror. Nonetheless, none of it seemed tangible or authentic.

The mirthful cackle of the ancient woman pierced the eerie silence, as she spoke, "Excellent, you can perceive them. These are harmless. It's the ones that have yet to arrive that concern us." She paused, fixing a steely gaze upon Red. "You may not be aware of this, but you are of noble lineage, tracing back to a time immemorial. Despite most dismissing the notion that any of the present royals possess even an iota of their forebears' genetic material, you were destined to be our offering. Alas, something went awry, and here we are."

"What have you done to me?" inquired Red, a sense of panic engulfing him.

"You are now a spirit, unencumbered by the desires of the flesh, such as hunger, thirst, or fatigue. No weakness shall ever assail you," replied the old crone.

"But if I desired to leave, could you not stop me?" queried Red, hoping for a glimmer of hope.

The aged woman chuckled heartily. "The other spirit I infused within you shall prevent any such endeavor. Your fates are intertwined, for he has a purpose, and now so do you. One."

As if on cue, a gust of wind whistled past the modest abode, followed by an intense wave of heat that permeated every corner. The crone fixed Red with a steely glare. "Do your job," she commanded, pointing towards the entrance.

Red regarded her with trepidation before turning towards the door. With each step, he felt the searing heat radiating from the doorknob, but he felt no pain. Once outside, he was met with an astonishing sight, the petite domicile besieged by towering infernos. What was he supposed to do? He pondered, unsure of what was expected of him.

A colossal figure of flames strode forward, addressing Red. "Step aside, Galangal," he intoned.

"What is that?" inquired Red, regarding the towering inferno with awe.

"You are that which you are. Do you not know?" boomed the towering figure, incredulous.

"I don't," admitted Red, feeling a tinge of embarrassment. "Am I supposed to fight you guys?"

The towering inferno laughed heartily, his booming voice echoing across the expanse. "You seem unaware of your identity, so how would you vanquish us?"

Within Red, a transformation occurred, and unshakeable confidence filled him as the rain cascaded down in sheets. But even as the deluge raged, the giants blazed on, their flames searing hot and unrelenting. Yet, Red smiled, a malicious grin spreading across his features as a legion of shades emerged from the earth. Two colossal shades materialized beside him, and in unison, they spoke with reverence, "Master."

As dark wisps wafted about them, Red felt a potent, malevolent energy growing within him, a force that he couldn't help but relish. The giant of fire looming over him demanded, "Why are you smiling?"

Red's smile faded, and he calmly asked, "Do you concede?"

The giant scoffed and lunged at Red with a blazing spear. But Red did not flinch, and just before the spear struck him, the giant and his weapon crumbled to ash, washed away by the torrential rain. The remaining giants charged at him, but the shades encircled them, suffocating their flames until they all vanished into the darkness.

Looking around, Red saw only shadows where the giants had stood moments before. "They have failed and called on us once again," one of the massive shades hissed. "I have never done this before."

"This is the first time," Red replied.

"It is you who made us master," the shade insisted.

"No, I did not," Red protested.

"Yes, you did," the shade countered. "We have protected them for centuries. Every 37 years, they fail, and we are called until they find a tithe. You were not their tithe, and they have rebirthed you many times. After each tithe, they are restored, and you are reborn. Most times, you remember."

"This time, I didn't," Red declared, though he sensed vague, disjointed memories stirring within him, the knowledge he hadn't possessed before.

Red questioned the purpose of their servitude, "Why do we do this for them?" he asked. The shade replied, "We are bound by the innards they possess, and so are you. She is a powerful witch, and her kind's practices can control and manipulate your lineage. When she has made you spirit, you remember all and are filled with rage, but it is too late by then - she has your guts and brain." Red persisted, "But why does it work if I am a spirit now?" The shade explained, "It's what she does that makes it work."

Red understood, "I will be rebirthed after they find their tithe. Then, 37 years from then, they will find me to create a whole scene, gut me, and I will be back here with you protecting them until they find a tithe again and again. That's crazy!" Red exclaimed. He wondered, "Where do all of you go?" The shade responded, "We rest and await you, sir." Red questioned, "What did we do before this trap?" The shade replied, "We don't remember anymore."

Filled with rage, Red walked back to the small house. As he did, his shoes burned off his feet and he scorched the ground beneath him. Darkness smoldered around him. The door flung open of its own accord.

Donny detested funerals and family gatherings. They were incredibly rich and bizarre. They possessed items that no one on Earth had ever seen, and they were priceless. It was his grandpa's funeral - the richest and strangest of them all.

On Donny's birthday, his grandpa asked him what he wanted. Donny told him, and he got up and went for a nap. When he came out of his room, he had what Donny had requested. Donny thought he had snuck out of his window or something.

During the funeral, Donny sat between his aunt and his dad. His aunt and uncle appeared to be in a heated, whispered-yell conversation. They were talking about something that belonged to grandpa - a ring, perhaps. Donny couldn't catch it, but he remembered him wearing a massive ring. With colors strange and ever-changing, and a constant smoldering aura, Donny had always thought the ring was imbued with magic. After the funeral, he and the rest of the family retreated to the estate for food, drink, and the reading of the will. Though Donny hadn't been particularly close to his grandfather, they had shared some enjoyable conversations in the past. Standing alone in a corner with a stiff drink, Donny was content to let the other guests come to him.

As the night progressed and Donny became increasingly buzzed, he found himself approaching groups of people and engaging in conversation. Perhaps they weren't as unbearable as he had previously thought. But then a bell rang, signaling the reading of the will. Donny didn't want to sit and listen to someone talk about things that had nothing to do with him, but he reluctantly made his way to the back of the room to wait it out.

The reading went on for about twenty minutes, and Donny could barely hear what was being said. Then, to his surprise, he thought he heard his name mentioned. His grandfather's ring was held up, and it was announced that he had wanted Donny to have it. Everyone in the room nodded in agreement, but Donny couldn't understand why his grandfather would have given him the ring. Feeling uncomfortable with all the attention, he got up and left the room, his parents following shortly after.

His parents were shocked to hear that Donny had been given the ring. They offered to hold onto it for him, but Donny refused. He continued drinking, feeling like the other guests were looking at him differently. Suddenly, the man who had read the will approached him and offered him private information. Donny followed him to another room, where the man handed him a closed envelope before quickly departing.

Donny opened the envelope to find a letter from his grandfather. It revealed that the ring had been taken from one of his dreams and that it had the power to help Donny achieve his goals. By wearing it to sleep, he could learn to be lucid and become more aware of what he wanted. But the letter ended with a warning: "Trust no one."

Donny stood in awe, his mind racing with confusion and wonder. Yet, he couldn't deny the fact that he was also quite intoxicated, the free liquor flowing freely into his system. As he delved deeper into the envelope, his fingers trembling with anticipation, he finally retrieved the ring. It was as he remembered it - smoldering black and white, emitting a strange smoke or some other unknown substance. Donny was mesmerized by its enigmatic beauty.

Suddenly, a sharp knock on the door startled him from his trance. It was the aunt who had been sitting next to him. "Hey Donny, how are you doing? Are you coming to join the other room soon? We are missing you out there," she said.

Donny's head snapped towards her, skepticism creeping into his voice. "Come on, you're messing with me," he said.

"No, really, come on Donny, I saved a dance for you," she said, her voice laced with kindness.

Donny shrugged and followed her into the other room, where he was met with the curious gazes of the other partygoers. It seemed that no one had noticed him before, but now all eyes were fixated on him. Grandpa's words echoed in his mind - it looked like no one here could be trusted. Nevertheless, he played along, allowing his aunt to grab him and lead him onto the dance floor. Despite his reservations, Donny found himself having fun.

Suddenly, the doors burst open, and a menacing figure strode in. "This ends here and now!" he bellowed. The old woman cackled and grasped his insides, causing Red to double over in agony.

"You will have it all and love it. You will protect us until we have found a tithe," she hissed, her words echoing throughout the room.

Red crawled towards the open door, knowing that the shades were waiting outside, unable to cross the threshold. The pain gradually subsided, and Red managed to get to his feet. The old woman sneered at him, calling him a "good watchdog" before slamming the door shut.

Minutes later, the old woman and her accomplices climbed into a truck and drove off, surrounded by a few of the shades. Red watched as they left the property, a sense of unease settling in the pit of his stomach.

As he turned back to the party, Donny couldn't shake the feeling that something was off. The people around him seemed strange and otherworldly, but he was too drunk to care. Even his parents were handing him drinks, their faces twisted into grotesque masks of ecstasy.

Suddenly, the main doors burst open, and a regal trio entered the room - Lady Charlotte, Prince Malice, and Princess Kalmmon. The room fell silent, and everyone bowed in deference. Donny recognized Lady Charlotte as his grandfather's sister, but something was off about her. She hadn't been at the funeral, and she didn't look as old as she should have.

Drunk and disoriented, Donny stumbled over to a corner and sank into a large armchair, watching as the others danced and laughed. But they wouldn't let him be - they yelled and cajoled him to join in the festivities. Even Princess Kalmmon herself called out to him, her eyes flashing with an alluring spark.

The old woman noticed the special attention Donny was receiving and leaned over to whisper in Prince Malice's ear. "He is the one," she said, her voice dripping with malice.

Malice nodded in agreement, and Princess Kalmmon danced closer to Donny, her movements becoming more and more provocative. They danced, laughed, and drank until it was time for Charlotte and Malice to bid their farewells. Kalmmon then turned to Donny and proposed that they continue the revelry at her abode, promising that they could obtain whatever they desired. "Ya man, for sure I'm in," Donny replied with a smile. "Ok, come on let's go," Kalmmon giggled, leading the way.

Donny informed her that he needed to bid his own parent's adieu first, but Kalmmon was insistent that he needed not to do so. "No, you don't. Come on, let's go. We got moonshine at home," she pressed. Donny shrugged and followed her, unnoticed by the others. He joined Kalmmon in the back of her truck as they departed for her house, where the journey proved to be longer than he had hoped. Nonetheless, Kalmmon managed to keep him engaged in conversation.

Upon their arrival, Donny and Kalmmon followed the old woman and Malice into the house, and Donny was too inebriated to notice the shades that surrounded them, nor the presence of Red, who was some distance away. "Will he be their tithe?" Red inquired of the shade beside him. "I think so, sir," the shade responded. "Well, that was fast," Red commented, to which the shade replied, "It was, sir, however, it is not over yet." "No, I guess not," Red mused.

"Sit, sit," the old woman beckoned as Donny, Kalmmon, and Malice obliged. Charlotte returned with a large, clear jar filled with a crystal-clear liquid. "You're going to love this," she laughed, handing the jug to Donny. He took a large swig, and it burned like hell, leaving him gasping for air. Nevertheless, he managed to regain his composure and proceeded to down more shots of the harsh beverage. Even his grand-aunt was partaking in the revelry.

Kalmmon switched on some music, which Donny found difficult to decipher due to his drunken state. Nevertheless, he danced with Kalmmon, and even Charlotte and Malice joined in. Eventually, the music was lowered, and they all sat down to converse. Donny was drunk, but he felt he still had some reserves left in the tank.

"Did you know your grandad used to come out to this land by himself for years until he found that ring you have, you have it don't you?" the old woman inquired. Donny nodded. "He used to tell me wild stories. I asked if I could come and see, and he said that I could not. One day, I followed him. He had not seen me, so I figured I would see what he had told me. But when I caught up to where he was, he was gone. I no longer knew where he was. I searched and searched until it was dark, and yet still did I search. In my search, I came across a small cabin with a light on. Maybe they had seen my brother. The cabin was camouflaged with shrubs, vines, and moss. I walked toward the cabin, and as I got close, I noticed a wolf was near the house." As I beheld its presence, it also beheld me. Its eyes bore the hue of blood, and from them flowed streams of crimson. A deafening howl escaped its lips and the cabin door parted ways, revealing a raven-haired woman with eyes as dark as the void. She called out to me, inquiring if I had lost my way. Overwhelmed by her mere presence, I remained silent. She beckoned me closer, assuring me that the wolf, which had now departed, would not harm me. "Come in for a bit," she said, "and then Persephone shall lead you to the terrain you know." Entranced, I accepted her invitation and entered her abode, a place adorned with fascinating curiosities. Sitting upon a chair hewn from a tree that resembled a throne, I was offered milk and cookies, while Alexandria spoke of my brother's frequent visits to her domain. She divulged that her land held no legends, and only a select few had ever ventured there, rarely returning to recount their experiences. Nevertheless, she was convinced that my brother frequented her domain and that he could lead us to a place that her late husband had believed to be present.

Though Alexandria had never seen this place, she was keen on discovering it. I had no answers to offer her, and yet, she remained unfazed. After bidding her farewell and thanking her for her hospitality, I made my way outside, where the wolf awaited me. It led me to an area that felt familiar and then departed. I knew I would face punishment for my late return, but your grandad spoke in my defense, claiming that he and I had ventured out to explore and that I had gotten lost. However, things changed after that day. As the house shook and the lights flickered, Donny grew anxious. The shade and Red recognized the imminent danger, realizing that they were facing a real and menacing creature, rather than a mythical one. He instructed his horde of shades to follow their instincts or face certain doom. The being that confronted them shone with the brilliance of the sun, its three faces resembling a bull, a ram, and a lion. It wore a gold beast plate adorned with peculiar markings and a red stone, while three crowns hovered above its heads. Its feet were hooves, and its hands were talons. Despite Red's attempts to subdue the creature's radiance, it only grew stronger, vaporizing some of the shades.

"The old woman and the two with her are all I seek," spoke the creature with a voice like a hurricane.

Red stepped forth with measured deliberation, his voice low and even. "I would let you pass, I really would," he said, "but I am bound to her. I cannot permit you to proceed."

Donny's nerves were on edge, his ears attuned to every sound that drifted in from outside. Rising from his seat, he announced, "I am going to take a look. It sounds insane out there." Kalmmon attempted to dissuade him, urging him to remain seated, but Donny brushed her off. "No, I'm going out there," he declared, slipping a hand into his pocket and inadvertently donning the ring.

As he opened the door, he was met with a sight that filled him with terror. Reacting instinctively, he shouted at the creature, "Get out of here!" To his surprise, the monster complied, disappearing into the night. Malice and Kalmmon pulled him back inside and bolted the door shut.

The shades were equally confounded by the bizarre turn of events. "We have never encountered such a creature," they murmured. "We thought he was the tithe," Red added. "Now we are unsure of what is unfolding."

After being given a stiff drink, Donny questioned the veracity of what he had witnessed. "Was that real or did you spike the shine and I am hallucinating?" he asked. The old woman placated him, insisting that nothing entered their domain without their consent.

"Don't give me that," Donny retorted, his pulse racing. "That thing looked malevolent!"

Despite Charlotte's attempts to speak, Donny was too agitated to listen. Malice, growing impatient, struck him hard on the back of the head, rendering him unconscious. "Why did you do that?" Charlotte demanded, to which Malice tersely replied, "It's time to go."

Dragging Donny to the truck, Malice flung him unceremoniously into the back and clambered in beside Charlotte and Kalmmon. As they drove away, Red pondered his role in the strange events unfolding around him.

"Can I leave this land?" he inquired of the shades. "No," they replied. "We are charged with safeguarding this property. However, we do occasionally accompany them on their travels to ensure their safety. But if the situation proved too perilous, we would intervene."

Determined to aid his compatriots, Red launched himself into the inky darkness, traversing the night sky until he alighted upon their location. They were headed for the very house where he had been wounded and his friend slain.

The truck came to a halt, and Charlotte instructed her minions to dispose of the bodies in the backyard while she made preparations in the north wing. As Malice and Kalmmon went about their grisly task, Red hovered above them, watching their every move.

But as Malice returned to retrieve Donny, he discovered that the young man had vanished. "Ma, we have a problem," he cried, bursting into the west wing. "He's gone!" Enraged, Charlotte berated Malice for his incompetence, warning him of the dire consequences that would befall them all if they failed to locate Donny. With Kalmmon in tow, Malice set out to find him.

The darkness parted as Red swept Donny up in its folds, whisking him away to some unknown destination. When Donny awoke, he found himself back at the old woman's house, though this time he was in the yard with a fearsome, flame-haired individual surrounded by a swarm of dark spirits. Donny was overcome with panic. "What's happening?" he exclaimed in a frantic voice.

"Well, Donny my boy, you're supposed to be their sacrifice, to someone," Red replied. "I was meant to be that someone, but as luck would have it, they ended up dead. Now, these three have one more chance, and you are that chance. But I am not willing to let that happen," he added, his tone steely. "Besides, perhaps you can be of help to me as well."

"How did you do what you did to that mighty creature?" Red inquired, his eyes fixed on Donny.

"I have no idea," Donny replied, shrugging his shoulders. He stood there in silence for a moment, fumbling in his pockets until he felt the ring. "Maybe it was this," he said, producing the ring. "I got it from my grandpa. He said it had strange power and that he pulled it from a dream."

"That's quite intriguing," Red remarked. "May I take a closer look?"

"Of course," Donny replied, handing the ring to Red. Red held the ring aloft, allowing the moonlight to reflect off its surface. As he did, strange beams of light emanated from the stone on the ring, swirling and jumping out with a greenish hue as if they were sparks.

Red was captivated by the light show, but then something caught his eye. He saw an illuminated green gate as he moved one of the beams of light across the forest. "Do you see that?" he asked Donny.

"I do, but I can't believe it," Donny replied. "This night has been quite a trip."

Without hesitation, Red and Donny made their way toward the gate, with Red holding the ring to keep it visible. The gate was much larger than they had anticipated, but they were undeterred. Red grabbed the handle, and as he handed the ring back to Donny, his hand fell through the air as if there was nothing there.

Donny reached out and grabbed the gate's handle. "I can see it, but I can't touch it now," he said. "Let's try this." He gave the ring back to Red, and both of them were able to touch the gate when they had it.

As they opened the gate and peered inside, they saw a forest that was different from the one they had just left. It had a greenish hue that seemed to blanket everything. "Are we going in?" Donny asked.

"I have nothing to lose," Red replied.

"Me neither," Donny added. "But you know what? This could be the place my grandpa used to come to when he was a young man, or so Charlotte said. And that would be cool, especially since it was the ring that showed us this gate."

As they continued to speak, they heard a vehicle approaching. "Let's go," Red said, and they hurriedly made their way into the gate. With the slamming of the gate, Donny and Red found themselves in a realm far beyond their own. They turned to behold a world of vibrant life, where even the trees and rocks appeared animated. What Donny initially mistook for small birds, were actually fairies, while the larger winged creatures revealed themselves to be harpies, who mocked and taunted them mercilessly.

After following a dirt path that led to a stone path and a building, Donny noticed a sweet aroma in the air as they entered. The doors shut behind them, and they discovered the room to be filled with an impressive collection of books, scrolls, and manuscripts, all suspended in the air against the walls, towering at least twenty feet high. The ceiling extended upwards in a spiral, and the room itself stretched a hundred feet long.

At the end of the room sat an old man in a large chair, lost in his book. As Donny and Red approached, the man slowly lifted his head and greeted them with a simple "Hi boys." To Donny's amazement, the man was his grandfather, who confirmed that he had been living beyond the gates.

When the old man turned to Red, he identified him as his brother, despite Red's confusion and lack of recognition. As Red struggled to comprehend the situation, Donny's grandfather seemed to stir something within him, a feeling of familiarity that he could not quite place.

With all eyes on him, Red shared the knowledge he had been given by his shades. He revealed that the old woman and others had made a deal with some unknown entity, requiring them to provide an offering every 37 years. This "tithe," as they called it, granted them power, but they failed to meet the deadline each time. The shades have speculated that they intended to enslave me. Something went awry, however, and I cannot recall what transpired. The woman killed me and transformed me into what I am now. I am to safeguard her from the consequences of her transgressions while she searches for a new tithe," Red said. "She is your sister, Charlotte, pops," Donny revealed.

The old man lowered his hands and remained motionless for a moment before breaking into a smile. "Allow me to show you something about this place, boys," he said. "What do you think of this apple in my hand?" he inquired as he presented it. "You don't," Donny began but cut himself off when he saw that his grandfather was indeed clutching an apple. "Take a bite," he urged, tossing the fruit to Donny. The latter examined it before taking a bite. "It's delicious!" he exclaimed.

"Indeed it is," the elder acknowledged, "but there is a dark side to this place as well." He then asked for a milkshake, which he received instantly in a steel cup. "Look inside," he instructed the boys. They peered in and saw dung and maggots, which quickly changed into a handheld vacuum cleaner. "You can never demand or tell, nor should you ever ask," he explained. "Instead, say it as though it is a fact. Watch," he added before requesting that the vacuum cleaner be removed. Nothing happened. "Say it as though you expect it to happen or to be there. 'I am so happy this vacuum cleaner is gone,'" he directed, and the device vanished. The boys were awestruck.

"Regarding this situation, Julian, I attempted to locate you, but I was unsuccessful. Perhaps now, with you here, we can discover you together," he said, addressing Red. "I discovered this place many years ago and developed a close relationship with the King, Queen, and wise men. They forged this ring in a dream, and when I awoke, I was wearing it. I made my father an affluent man, but he, like the rest of them, was overcome by greed and contempt. Although I used my power to make more wealth, which came naturally to me, they did not adopt the same habits. I also made you, Charlotte, Violet, and Ben very wealthy. But it was insufficient for you all. Charlotte began delving into some bizarre activities, and that is when I stopped seeing her. That is when you vanished," he revealed.

"I attempted to appease you all and gave you this," he said, producing a crystal with a blackish-red liquid inside. "It granted you all immortality, but as I have aged, I have realized that it was a grave error. Drinking it was akin to consuming hell," Red remarked, recalling his memory of imbibing it. "Yes, it was," the elder chuckled.

"You recall his words," Red intoned, a sudden burst of memory illuminating his face. Donny's grandfather stood before them, surveying the vast expanse of books that surrounded them. "I am truly grateful that all I need to know is contained in this tome," he murmured, plucking a volume from the very air. Turning to face the others, he queried, "Do you concur?" Their agreement was immediate and earnest.

Opening the book, the aged patriarch began to peruse its contents, while Donny and Red waited with barely concealed impatience. After what seemed like an eternity, he looked up, his eyes alight with a newfound comprehension. Though the revelation had crushed him, he now possessed the knowledge to remedy the situation.

At last, Donny spoke. "Well?" The others nodded expectantly. "Are you ready to impart the truth?"

With a heavy heart, the old man began to speak. "It seems that the more wealth you amassed, the more bizarre you became. Charlotte made a pact with a being called the Chronicle, including all of you. When the time came to fulfill the bargain, however, you were unable to deliver the tithe. They killed you, but because you are immortal, the tithe was not fulfilled."

He paused, then continued, "But that was not your only mistake. You failed to read the fine print, my brother. In the event of a broken oath, the defaulter becomes a dark protector until a new tithe is procured. You have but three days to provide this tithe, or all shall perish at the hands of the Chronicle."

The gravity of the situation was not lost on Donny or Red, and they both stared at the old man with a mixture of horror and fascination. "This has been going on for centuries," the patriarch continued, his voice heavy with sorrow. "Every thirty-seven years, the tithe is due. But what I cannot fathom is why all of you were seeking more than wealth and immortality. What else were you hoping to gain?"

Red shook his head in despair. "I do not know."

"I thought you had left of your own volition," the old man muttered. "But instead, you lived for thirty-seven years, died, and were reborn for another thirty-seven, only to be used again and again. And my sister is at the heart of it all." He laughed bitterly. "She is a powerful woman, but even she has never discovered this place, despite living on the same land as the gate."

Donny spoke up, "When I was at her house earlier, before everything became strange, she spoke only of you. I believe she desires this place, or perhaps the ring."

The old man nodded. "Or both," he said darkly. "But why all this power? And despite all the resources I gave her, why does she live in such poverty? What has she spent her wealth on?"

Donny had one more question. "Why did you give me the ring, anyway, Pops?"

His grandfather chuckled, "I am certain that you will fare much better with the ring than I did during my time with it," he remarked, prompting Donny to smile in gratitude. "There is much more to that ring than what I wrote to you in the letter," he continued. "If you can find it to be within darkness yet in the full brightness of the sun, you will be able to do or create whatever your mind can conceive in the waking world. The entire time I had the ring in my possession, I was not able to create those conditions. I believe you will figure this out, as it is not recorded in these books nor is it possible to be. There do seem to be rules of sorts."

Donny pondered this momentarily before asking, "Is that why she didn't take it from me while I was unconscious?"

"Indeed," his grandfather replied. "No one can hold it in their hand unless you give them permission to do so."

"That makes sense. How could Red hold it, then?" Donny mused.

"Who is Red?" the old man inquired.

"That would be me, but I guess I am your brother, Julian," Red revealed.

The old man erupted in laughter. "No, no. 'Red' is a perfect name for you, my brother. It suits the body that you have. Red it is."

"How could our sister do that to you for so long? What is so important that she has done all this?" the old man pondered. "Whatever the case, we must go see the king," he declared. With that, he put the book down and exclaimed, "Aren't you glad that we can fly here?" before leaping up into the air.

Donny and Red exchanged a look before following suit. This time, they were successful in their flight, even though Donny was still shaky. They arrived at a massive castle with a grand garden featuring a full orchard and vineyard. It was breathtaking. Upon landing, they were greeted by a majestic older man with a white beard and kingly robes. There was a ring on every finger, including his thumbs, and a fiery intensity behind his eyes.

"Ah, Al, it looks like you have brought visitors," the king remarked. "It's been so long since I have seen a new face around here."

"Yes, great king. I have with me my grandson and my brother, however, my brother is under a strange curse done by my sister, Charlotte," the old man explained. "Many years has she tried to find your home," Red said. "What manner of curse is this?" the king inquired, piqued with curiosity. "Follow me," he continued, leading the group off the beaten path, through a stone door, and into a labyrinth. After navigating the maze and reaching the center, the king grabbed Red's head and probed deeper. Suddenly, Red was gone, transported back to Charlotte's front yard with his shades enveloping him. "Master, they are here," one of the shades muttered. Red inquired as to what they were up against and was greeted with a terrifying sight: gigantic beasts that he could never have imagined in his wildest dreams. Fueled by a burning rage, Red summoned his powers and launched an assault on the beasts. He was getting the hang of his powers, but he despised being bound by his grand Aunt.

"Where did he go?" Donny asked. "It would seem that he was needed at my sister. She must have been under attack," Donny's grandpa replied. The king suggested that they search the mazes for the man with the answers. They walked and talked until they came upon a small shrine, and the king bowed before it. The shrine started to move, revealing steps leading down, and the group descended. As they reached the bottom of the stairs, a man was floating horizontally in the air, seemingly asleep. The room was bare, except for the mysterious figure. "You know why we are here," the king declared. "Yes, yes, I do," replied the man as he turned over and descended to the ground. "Sit," he ordered. They obediently sat down in a circle on the ground.

The man drew a symbol on the floor, and the ground beneath it cracked open, revealing a large crystal that shone like the ocean and swirled like it too. It was a captivating sight. The man peered into the crystal and saw Red. "You have had a long, torturous life, my friend," he said, before turning to Al. "This is not a difficult fix. There are two ways to approach this, each with different outcomes. The first is to wait until they make their tithe, and then he will be reborn, which will allow us to find him quickly. Alternatively, the second option is immediate but not ideal. He will remain a creature of darkness, not fully human, but humanish."

"Well, what is it?" the king inquired.

"If we prevent them from making the tithe, they will either be killed or left powerless. We will burn his innards along with the brain so that he may never be bound again," he replied. "Alternatively, we could destroy the ones that make the tithes too," Donny suddenly interjected. All fell silent, considering the proposal.

"Red is powerful, but he is bound," Al said thoughtfully.

"Yes, but I am not," Donny declared. "Pops, what else can this ring do?" The king, his grandpa, and the other man could not contain their amusement and broke into laughter. After a while, the man who had been suspended in the air began to speak. "My name is Ulumba. The king and I founded this place and unlocked the power within. We have been living here for as long as we can remember, unraveling its secrets." The king cleared his throat, drawing the man's attention. "Well, we have been here ever since, but it is not ours." He continued, "This is where dreams sleep or where they wander when they slumber. It's a long and complex story, but your ring is a much shorter one."

"For some inexplicable reason, your grandpa could see the gate during the day. He stepped through, and we got to know him and taught him about this place. But one day, he stopped coming. So, we entered his dreams and crafted a ring that would enable him to extract things from dreams and bring them into reality while awake. See it, say it, and it shall be," he explained.

Donny inspected the ring in his hand with wonder. "You did a great job of acting normal when you could have done anything you wanted," he said. His grandpa hung his head in regret. "Yeah, except find my brother," he said.

Donny tried to comfort him. "Come on pops, we found him now, right? Maybe not in the best circumstances, but still," he said. His grandfather agreed. "You're right," he said.

Ulumba asked, "What is it that you plan to do?" AL smiled, saying, "We should leave and ask my brother what he would prefer." "Yes, I agree," Donny chimed in. The king and the other man shrugged their shoulders. "Okay, but if you need our help, do not hesitate to come to get us," the king said. Both Donny and his grandfather nodded.

Suddenly, Donny exclaimed, "I see the gate!" and they were standing before it. Donny was startled; he had to get used to these strange happenings, he thought. They opened the gate and stepped through. It was still night, and they could see Red and his shades lurking around the house. The shades noticed them and started to take them away to Red, but Donny stopped them. "Please, we don't want Charlette to know we are here. Bring Red here instead," he said.

But before they could reach Red, a fierce battle broke out. Three giants, made of what looked like diamonds, were swinging at the shades that swirled around them. Red rose into the air, growing to an enormous size. His eyes were a deep crimson, filled with rage.

The behemoth figures charged towards Red, but he merely opened his arms and a swath of inky blackness poured forth. The shadows coalesced into the form of massive dragons, which peeled away from Red and shot toward the giants. The dragons encircled them, battling fiercely as they soared through the air. After a brief scuffle, they entwined themselves around the giants and plummeted deep into the earth's core. The giants exploded upon impact, shaking the ground beneath Donny and Al's feet.

Red's gaze shifted to the two men. "What's the plan?" he asked, his voice rumbling like thunder. Donny and Al explained their strategy and conferred with the mighty being for a moment. "My shades say they are out gathering a tithe right now," Red revealed. "We can intercept them when they return."

Donny was taken aback. "We thought they were already here!"

"No, they're on their way," Red clarified. "My shades and I are attuned to one another. You need to hide. Let me help you."

With a flick of his wrist, a cloak of impenetrable darkness enshrouded Al and Donny. The veil allowed them to see through but remained impervious to prying eyes. Red returned to his post while his shades observed Charlotte's movements.

"They're here," the shades announced to Red, who nodded in response. Charlotte and her cohort appeared, with Malice carrying an additional captive over his shoulder. Donny rushed over to Red.

"They're going to start fast, she doesn't waste any time," Donny cautioned.

Red's deep laugh boomed through the air. "I'm well aware of that," he replied.

As Red, Al, and Donny dashed up to the porch, the door slammed shut with a resounding thud. "Neither I nor my shades can pass the threshold," Red declared with a somber tone. "Then it falls to us, Gramps," Donny asserted, turning to his grandfather for guidance. The elderly man nodded and offered a small smile. "It appears that way," he acknowledged. Despite Red's discontent, he and his shades encircled the porch while Donny and Al took hold of the doorknob and stepped inside.

However, upon entering the room, they discovered that it was devoid of any human presence. Red approached the door and realized that the field that had previously obstructed him from entering the house was absent. Without feeling any pain, Red walked into the main room where Donny and Al had congregated. "Where did they go?" Donny inquired, perplexed. "I'm afraid I have no answer," Red and Al responded in unison. The three stood there silently, their surroundings engulfed in confusion.

Suddenly, a thought occurred to Red. "Perhaps my shades could locate them," he suggested. Calling out to them, Red directed his shades to search for Charlotte and her companions. Despite their efforts, they couldn't detect her signature. "They can't find her," Red disclosed. "Now what?" Donny asked, feeling somewhat helpless. "Although they failed to sense her, I'll send them out to scour the forest for any signs of her whereabouts," Red resolved. "An excellent idea," Al commended.

Subsequently, Red dispatched his shades, while he and the others waited outside for their return. After a brief period, they reappeared, and Red inquired, "What did you discover?" "Master, they're two miles south, deep in the woods," Red's shades reported. "There's an odorless, smokeless fire burning behind a small, overgrown cabin." Without hesitation, Red gestured for Donny and his grandfather to follow him into the darkness as they set out to find Charlotte and her group.

Donny's ring glowed with an ethereal light that was just enough for him and his grandfather to see the path before them. The two walked silently, their eyes locked on the dimly lit cabin that lay ahead of them. As they approached, the structure seemed eerily deserted. But then, as if by some magic, the illusion shimmered and they could see Charlotte and her companions standing there, along with a majestic woman draped in multiple layers of regal attire. In front of them lay the tithe, resting on a massive stone between the woman and the fire. Suddenly, the tithe began to levitate into the air.

"We must hurry," Donny urged.

"Of course," his grandfather replied.

They slowly moved forward, but as they approached, the wolf Persephone caught their scent and blocked their way. A voice commanded them to come forward. Reluctantly, the wolf yielded, allowing them to pass. As they drew nearer, Donny realized that Kalmmon and Malic were no longer with the group.

"You are trespassing," the woman snarled, glaring at them.

"Enough of the theatrics. This ends now, Charlotte," Al said, interrupting her.

Charlotte smiled wickedly. "You're alive, brother. How can this be?"

"I never died, Charlotte. I simply left," he replied.

"Oh, you went there, did you? To the place you never showed me," she retorted. "But now, brother, I don't need you or your hidden places. I have power of my own, and soon, I will claim my rightful seat, with or without you," she declared.

As they listened to her words, Malice sneaked up behind Al and hit him hard on the head, causing him to crumple to the ground. Red attempted to leap into action but found himself frozen in place. He shifted his gaze to Charlotte, who was gripping a bloody burlap pouch that she had tied to her hip. As she clutched it, she muttered strange words, and Red felt himself lift into the air, completely immobilized.

He hung there, suspended in the air, unable to move as Red struggled to free himself from the woman's spell. Donny rushed over to his grandfather, who lay motionless on the ground, Malice looming over him like a vulture waiting to feast on carrion. "Get out of the way," Donny yelled, but Malice merely shrugged and went back to where the others were standing.

"What of the boy with the ring?" the majestic woman asked, her voice carrying a note of interest.

Donny's heart sank as he realized that his grandfather was gone. Tears streamed down his face as he wished he knew how to use the ring better. If only he had been able to master its power, he would show them all.

"Hand me the ring, boy," the woman said, her hand outstretched.

"No, I will not," Donny said, his voice shaking with defiance.

"In the end, you will give it to me, so why not give it to me now?" the woman asked, her tone dripping with superiority.

"Why should I give it to you? I don't even know you," Donny said, his eyes fixed on the tithe resting on the large rock.

"I am Alexandria," she proclaimed. "I am the guide to power; only through me do any attain it."

"By giving a tithe to some sort of beast?" Donny asked, his voice incredulous.

"Yes, and she is no beast, she is very powerful," Alexandria said, a smug smile on her face.

As they spoke, Red struggled to figure out what he could do. He stretched the darkness from his feet into the ground, searching until he found the vacant bodies of the previous tithes. The darkness filled them and reanimated them, under Red's control.

While Donny and the woman talked, Charlotte heard a sound that made her heart race. She wasn't sure what it was at first, but then she heard the shuffling of feet. Two of the dead had grabbed her by the arms, and she struggled to break free. Malice hit them over the heads, but four more were there, grabbing at her.

Kalmmon was being attacked by three more of the dead that were filled with Red's power. Now Alexandria was no longer concerned with Donny, but with what was happening around her. She shot energy blasts at them and had gotten most of them, but not before one of them grabbed the pouch tied to Charlotte's hip and threw it into the fire.

All the reanimated bodies dropped as it burned, and Red burst into flames, quickly becoming ash.

Donny's head swiveled away from the disturbing scene before him, only to find that Alexandria had transformed into Ulumba, the man from the other side of the gate. His astonishment was palpable as he bellowed, "What?!" Ulumba chuckled under his breath before answering, "You see, lad when I entered the gate and dwelled in that realm, I acquainted myself with its creator. I desired to elevate her, so in short, I have been feeding her with human souls, and imbuing power upon individuals such as your grand-aunt. Nevertheless, that's not our endgame. My intention is to create an opening for her to extend her dominion into our world, and I will be at her side. We shall refashion this world according to our liking," Ulumba declared.

Suddenly, a fierce gust of wind appeared, whirling and twisting, extinguishing the flames. The darkness surrounding them gave way to an ebony rain, plummeting down in droplets that Donny perceived as black. As abruptly as it had begun, the rain ceased, and darkness crept across the ground, enshrouding Donny and his deceased grandfather. It encompassed them and then consumed them.

When Donny regained his senses, he realized that he was back on Charlotte's estate, with Red staring fixedly at him, and his grandfather lying motionless beside him. "Red, how did you arrive here?" Donny inquired. "I don't know, I was ablaze, then everything turned black, and I beheld myself. The strangest occurrence happened next; I walked into myself and recollected every moment, every year. Then I broke apart and fell as a downpour, and I was conscious of every drop that I was. I reassembled myself, took you and my brother, and transported you here," Red replied. Donny was dumbfounded. "What about my grandfather?" he inquired.

"I am pleased that you inquired, for in my recollections, I unearthed a place, a far-off place," Red spoke. Donny's resolve was unyielding. "Then let us go," he declared. Red was hesitant. "I am not certain how to transport us there," he admitted. Donny pondered for a moment before extending his hand. "Give me your hand," he said. Red reluctantly complied. Donny clutched his hand and spoke, "I am grateful that we can venture to the place within your thoughts." Their forms faded and vanished. When they materialized, the surroundings were pitch-black. Donny could only discern a glimmer of light from his ring, whereas Red's sight was not inhibited by the darkness. They found themselves in a diminutive cavern, concealed in the depths of the sea. The cavern took the shape of a water droplet, with a small pool of water at the center. "What do we do now?" Donny inquired. "Now, I take it from here, young man," Red responded, as he lifted Donny's grandfather's lifeless form and plunged into the pool. Red swam to the cavern floor and held Al while he dug a grave. Although it was a challenging task, Red had an easier time than most, as he was no longer entirely human. Once the hole was ready, he placed Al inside and covered it up, then swam back to the surface. "Now, we wait," Red said. "How long?" Donny asked, anxiety creeping in. "As long as it takes," Red replied. "But we cannot afford to wait, the tithe would have already been delivered," Donny pleaded. "Agreed, we must depart. Al will recover in due time, and we need not be here," Red stated. "But when he regains consciousness, he will be all alone," Donny fretted. "Nay, he will not. I shall leave some shades to keep watch over him," Red reassured him. "So, you are no longer bound to Charlotte?" Donny queried. "It appears that way. The other spirit that dwelt within me departed when I was incinerated. It seems that I am free... whatever I am," Red chuckled darkly. "Come, let us proceed, young Donny," Red beckoned. As they approached the area where Charlotte and the others were, they noticed that the ritual was already underway. This time, Ulumba was not in disguise. Without delay, Red darted towards the tithe, shrouding himself in his darkness and swiftly sweeping Ulumba away. However, a hand of light suddenly materialized and ensnared the darkness, forcefully yanking it back. A magnificent blue smoke dragon emerged from the air and grappled with the hand, but Red managed to escape into the night. Ulumba glared at Donny. "Where did you learn to do that?" he bellowed. Donny simply shrugged. Ulumba then fired energy at Donny, but it had no effect. The hand and dragon vanished into the darkness. Donny and Charlotte attempted to retaliate, but none of their efforts proved effective. They were at a stalemate, for their powers originated from the same source, rendering their spells and constructs nullified.

 Meanwhile, Red had taken the man designated as the tithe to a secure location and left him there. As he made his way back to Donny, one of his shades approached him. "The waters are agitated, sir," it reported. Red was conflicted. What should he do? He resolved to visit the cave, where the pool of water was softly bubbling. Suddenly, the water started to churn violently, and a brilliant white light radiated from within. The water swirled, and Al rose from the vortex, his eyes and mouth emanating energy. When he was completely above the pool, he looked at Red, but his eyes pierced right through him. Al blinked, and his eyes returned to their normal green hue, but a newfound spark ignited within them. "I'm sorry, my brother. I didn't know," Al apologized. "It's alright. I'm just happy to see you alive again," Red replied. "How did you know of this place?" Al inquired with a hint of amusement.

"Oh yes, I got incinerated," Red began, his voice heavy with the weight of his experience. "But somehow, I returned, and when I did, I could remember so much, Al. Things I couldn't imagine I knew, and this place was one of those memories. I was going to use this place to somehow fix my situation, but it can't work with me like this." His words trailed off, a hint of sadness and regret in his voice.

"What is this place? What am I now?" Al asked, his voice filled with confusion and uncertainty.

"Well, brother, there is a long story for that, and we really should hurry and see how your grandson is faring," Red suggested, a sense of urgency in his tone.

"Yes, of course. How do we leave?" Al asked, his voice tinged with impatience.

"However you want. You can go through it or just think of the last place you remember," Red replied.

Al closed his eyes and thought of what he saw before everything went black. In an instant, they were back and standing beside Donny.

"This is fruitless already!" Ulumba yelled, his frustration palpable. He was furious that they lost the tithe and that all their attempts to do anything to Donny were useless.

"Ulumba, you... how is this?" Al stammered out, surprised to see the woman he had encountered earlier now revealed as Ulumba.

"Keep up, old man!" Ulumba snapped. "I was the woman, but the illusion is lost, so here we are, caught up, Al."

"But why? You had everything anyone could want," Al said, struggling to understand.

"It wasn't real, Al. None of it. I want it here, where things are real. And by feeding her souls, I found that it's bringing her here. Her power is already here, Al. Your brothers and sisters all did it. Your own family is ushering her in and will be rewarded. Will you oppose us, Al?" Ulumba's voice was filled with a sense of greed and power-hunger.

Al couldn't believe what he was hearing. "Does the king know about this?" he asked.

Ulumba laughed. "That fool. He loves everything just the way they are. He is happy in his world of make-believe," Ulumba said.

As they spoke, a low, slow rumble came from the ground. At first, it was so slight that no one noticed, but then it was like energy came rising to the top, and when it did, it sounded like a sonic boom. Rocks started levitating, as did everyone standing there, caught up in the force of the rising power.

As soon as the levitation ceased, a sudden burst of white-blue light erupted from the colossal boulder. "There's no tithe," Ulumba cried out, but his words were cut short as Charlotte was snatched by the light and placed onto the rock. Malice and Kalmmon attempted to intervene but were forcefully dragged onto the boulder, only to be consumed by the light, leaving behind their lifeless corpses. Ulumba glowed like a golden sun, basking in the energy that had devoured the souls of his cohorts.

Donny muttered something under his breath, and the ground beneath them shook. Suddenly, two enormous hands made of stone and dirt emerged from the earth and grasped Ulumba, ripping him apart. Donny's grandfather looked at him in astonishment. "That was you, I am guessing," he said.

"Ya, but I don't want to do that again," Donny said.

"You won't have to, kid," Red said reassuringly. "We're here."

"It would have been nice to have known a little more about what we're dealing with, though," Donny's grandpa commented.

"But we do know where to go to find out," Red responded.

"That we do," Al agreed.

Red wrapped Donny in a shroud of darkness and swiftly carried him away. Al and Red soared through the air until they reached the spot where they believed the gate was located. However, they needed Donny's ring to locate it since Red couldn't see it, and Al no longer had the ability to sense it. Donny shone his ring along the edge of the forest. "There it is," he whispered.

Red and Al followed Donny to the gate and held onto him as they stepped through it.

As soon as they entered the gate, a putrid stench of decaying flesh assaulted their nostrils. Swarms of flies hovered above the corpses that littered the pathways, while the walls themselves seemed to pulsate with dead flesh. Donny's grandfather urged him to use his power to create something, but when Donny conjured an image of an apple in his hand, it transformed into a live cobra that tried to strike at him. Al warned them that they couldn't rely on that and they continued their search for the king, hoping that he could provide answers.

As they made their way through the desolate landscape, they discovered that even the gardens and the creatures that called them home had been consumed by the blight. Every living thing seemed to have been devoured by the ground, leaving nothing but desolation and the buzzing of flies.

Fearful of the consequences of trying to create anything else, they walked carefully through the existing buildings and pathways. But then they heard a faint singing or humming coming from beneath them. Following the sound, they ran to a small hut where Al promptly lifted a floor mat, revealing a hidden staircase beneath it. Red and Donny followed him down the stairs.

At the bottom, they found the king sitting among lush green plants, reading a book and seeming to have had a bit too much to drink. Al greeted him, then asked if he knew what was happening in his kingdom.

As they descended into the depths of the underground, the stench of decay grew thicker with each step they took. Swarms of flies buzzed around, feasting on the corpses that littered the walkways. The walls appeared to pulse with the sickening hues of dead flesh, giving the impression that the entire place was a living, breathing creature.

"Don't lose hope, boy," Donny's grandfather encouraged him. "Try to create something, anything. Maybe that will help us find a way out of this nightmare."

"I'm so glad I have this delicious apple in my left hand," Donny said, doing as he was told. In an instant, a writhing cobra head replaced the apple, its forked tongue darting out in search of prey.

"That's not what we need," Al said, visibly shaken by the horrific sight. "We'll have to keep searching for a way out."

As they walked, the group saw that even the gardens and animals had been stripped of life, reduced to nothing more than desiccated husks pasted to the ground. The only sound was the droning of flies as they buzzed around, filling the air with their incessant hum.

They walked carefully, avoiding any attempts at creation for fear of what they might conjure. Despite their caution, they soon heard a soft humming sound coming from below. Red's sharp senses led them to a small hut, where Al revealed a hidden staircase leading underground.

The group descended the steps, emerging in a room filled with thriving plants and the sight of the king, who appeared to have indulged in a few too many spirits.

"Gentlemen, it's good to see you," the king slurred. "I know what's happening here, and it's not good news. We're inside her body, and everything you see around you is her physical manifestation. We can't do anything about it."

"What do you mean, we can't do anything?" Donny asked incredulously.

"We can't leave," the king said, his voice tinged with sadness. "Her hordes are coming, and they'll kill us. We're like foreign invaders, and the body will reject us."

As if on cue, the ground shook, and a horde of nightmarish creatures burst through the floor. Red and Al fought with ferocity, while the king sneaked away, followed closely by Donny.

In a small room, Donny implored the king for information on how to use the ring, hoping to find a way out of their predicament.

"I'll tell you what you need to know, but I'm not sure it will help you," the king said, shrugging. "It'll at least take my mind off things for a bit."

Donny listened intently as the king shared his knowledge, then thanked him and ran back to join the fight.

"I know what to do!" Donny yelled to his comrades. "Meet me later!"

With that, Donny turned and sprinted back up the walkways toward the gate, his mind racing with a plan to save them all.

He deftly dodged the monstrous beasts that lurked in the darkness, their claws scraping against the fleshy walls as they attempted to seize him. "I glad to be at the gate," he muttered under his breath, fervently hoping that his desperate plan would succeed. However, when he arrived at his destination, it was not the gate that greeted him, but a damp, putrid chamber that seemed to pulsate with a sickening rhythm. Each contraction made the room feel smaller and more oppressive than before.

"I am at the castle!" he cried out, hoping beyond hope that the sound of his own voice would transport him to safety. And just as he wished, he found himself suddenly standing at the gate, he exited into the dense woods of his grand aunt Charlotte's land. Clutching the ring tightly in his hand, he held it up to the full moon, basking in its radiant glow until the ring began to emit a blinding light.

"At last," he exclaimed triumphantly. "I am grateful that my grandfather never discovered this gate when he was a child, for it never truly existed. The ring and the power it holds are mere illusions."

As the moon and the ring both glowed with a scorching intensity, a vortex of swirling colors opened up in the sky. A thin red strand plunged down to the earth like a needle, piercing the ground with a deafening crash. The strand then recoiled in a colossal explosion, and the sky closed with a deafening boom. Donny looked down at his hand and realized that the ring was gone.

He gazed up at the sky, and then, inexplicably, his vision started to blur and distort. He stumbled and fell, feeling as if he were plummeting through the ground until everything went black. Years passed, and then more years, until it was time for Donny's grandfather's funeral. He sat somberly between his father and his grand-uncle Julian, who had been his grandfather's inseparable companion. Despite his distaste for funerals, Donny was deeply fond of his grandfather.

After the service, there was a lavish feast with plenty of food and drink, befitting a family of Donny's stature.

Julian extended a glass to Donny, but Donny politely refused. While conversing with his grand-uncle, a lanky gentleman approached Donny. "Sir, may I have a moment of your time?" he inquired. Julian acknowledged the request and departed.

"Yes, of course. How may I assist you?" Donny responded. "Your grandfather instructed me to deliver this to you privately, sir," the man said, handing Donny a weighty envelope. Donny placed it in his suit pocket, expressed his gratitude, and made his way to the restroom. Once inside, he opened the envelope and discovered a peculiar ring and a letter. Reading the contents of the letter, he stared intently at the ring, and a rush of memories flooded his mind, causing a sense of terror to consume him. As he emerged from the bathroom, he was met with the gaze of the guests. "We made this for you. Isn't this sufficient?" they echoed in unison. Overwhelmed, Donny collapsed to the floor, unconscious. When he came to, he found himself lying on the bathroom floor with the letter and the ring beside him.

Ethereal Pirates: Bound by Fate

A succession of sleepless nights had left Paul's eyes bleary and fatigued, but an irresistible sense of proximity to something profound fueled his determination. His relentless research had led him on a whirlwind tour through realms both fantastical and uncharted, unearthing texts so extraordinary that they defied his prior knowledge. Paul wearied yet undeterred, rubbed his eyes and released a world-weary sigh before immersing himself once more in his pursuit of knowledge. Yet, as his eyes scanned the mystic verses, the very words seemed to ripple and vanish, plunging him into an abyss of darkness.

Within that inky void, a formidable trap materialized before him, while an awe-inspiring entity strode forth, apparently heedless of the peril that lay in its path. In an instant, the trap sprang to life, ensnaring the colossal being, and torrents of its ethereal blood flowed forth like galaxies spilling from cosmic wounds. A deafening roar reverberated with such seismic intensity that it threatened to rupture the very fabric of Paul's perception.

With a jolt, Paul's eyes snapped open, and he realized that sleep had claimed him, however fleetingly. As he sat in the afterglow of his surreal dream, he pondered its cryptic meaning. It seemed to echo the tantalizing secrets he tirelessly sought in his readings, further stoking his insatiable thirst for enlightenment.

Paul hailed from a lineage of antiquarians, a family history that traced its origins to a bygone era of swashbuckling ancestors who pillaged not for gold but for ancient texts harboring a unique form of treasure. Their extensive libraries, continually expanding, housed a wealth of knowledge waiting to be unlocked. However, it was the enigmatic revelations of his friend, Jeremy, an archaeologist whose recent discoveries had piqued Paul's curiosity, that had ignited his relentless quest. Jeremy's tales of intriguing findings from archaeological digs had become the catalyst propelling Paul into the world of manuscripts and ancient relics.

Finally acknowledging the need for rest, Paul reluctantly rose from his seat and made his way to his sleeping chamber, where the boundless mysteries of his dream continued to haunt his thoughts.

Paul's slumber was a turbulent maelstrom, an incessant whirlwind of chaotic senses, elusive fragments of dreams slipping through his grasp. Amid this nocturnal kaleidoscope, vivid, extravagant scenes intermingled with colossal and horrifying beings. He would jolt awake only to tumble back into the tumultuous realm of dreams, over and over, until finally, in one awakening, he found the strength to raise his head. His body was drenched, his skin ablaze with fever.

With a sense of urgency, he rose and sought solace beneath the frigid cascade of a cold shower, its icy embrace a respite from the searing heat that had gripped him. The sensation was invigorating, the cleansing waters washing away the lingering remnants of his disorienting dreams. Eventually, he stepped out and returned to his bed, sinking into a deep and uninterrupted slumber that stretched until the sun stood high in the sky. It was the ringing of his phone that roused him this time, and his father's voice on the other end.

"Paul, are you awake?" his father inquired.

"Yeah, I am," Paul replied. "What's going on, Dad?"

"You need to come over right away," his father insisted.

"What's so urgent, Dad?" Paul pressed for more information.

"Just get down here, Paul," his father replied before abruptly ending the call.

Perplexed but compliant, Paul readied himself and made his way to his father's residence. As he arrived, he was met by a grand and vibrant gathering, a massive party that seemed to engulf his father's vast estate. The wealth of Paul's family was nothing short of opulent, a mysterious fortune that had been passed down through the generations. No one had ever divulged the source of their affluence, and Paul, content in his solitary pursuits, had rarely inquired. However, it appeared that his solitude was no longer assured.

Every living relative seemed to have congregated on the premises, and Paul couldn't help but wonder what had transpired and why he had been left in the dark until this moment. He parked his car and began his approach toward the house, but before he could reach it, his father appeared, extending his arms in a welcoming gesture.

"Ah, son, you made it," his father exclaimed as he embraced Paul.

"Yeah, I did. What's going on here, Dad?" Paul inquired.

"Your mother didn't give you the message?" his father asked with a hint of surprise in his tone.

"No, Dad, she didn't. What is all this about?" Paul queried.

"Well, there are some family members from the old country who have decided to visit. They are the reason for our great wealth," his father explained. "Come and meet them."

Paul followed his father through the bustling crowd, their path winding its way toward an imposing table adorned with four enigmatic figures. These men seemed as if they were the embodiment of fire, their eyes ablaze with an otherworldly gleam, a tantalizing blend of mischief and raw power. Their movements were imbued with a sense of unbridled vitality as if they were untethered by the constraints of mere mortals. Paul stood transfixed, his curiosity piqued by this otherworldly presence. Who were these extraordinary individuals?

As his father approached the table, Paul followed, a palpable sense of being out of his element enveloping him. "May I introduce to you, great ones, my son, Paul," his father announced. With an air of trepidation, Paul stepped forward, an overwhelming feeling of welcome washing over him. The men's eyes sparkled with delight as they greeted him, and Paul couldn't help but respond with a beaming smile.

One of them, exuding an air of wisdom and mystery, addressed Paul, "So, your father tells me you've followed the family traditions.

However, if you stay late enough tonight, we might be able to enlighten you about some aspects you might not have known. Would this interest you, young Paul?"

Paul chuckled, "I'm not a young man, sir," he replied, "but yes, I would be quite interested."

"Good, I will enjoy that. For now, sit, eat, and drink with us," the man replied.

Paul's father swiftly secured a chair for his son at the illustrious table. The spread before them was a feast for the senses, an abundance of food and drink that beckoned to be indulged. "Feast, young Paul, and drink, for how long will you live if not now?" one of the four men cheered, prompting the rest to join in the revelry.

Inspired by their jubilant encouragement, Paul embraced the meal with the fervor of a ravenous beast, quaffing his drink as though he had never tasted such ambrosia in his life. A newfound vigor coursed through his veins, energizing him in a way he had never experienced before.

As the festivities unfolded, Paul marveled at how these enigmatic figures seemed to infuse the entire gathering with an electric energy. Laughter and merriment filled the air, and Paul found himself overwhelmed by the intoxicating atmosphere that surrounded him.

The lively soirée took an abrupt hush, and Paul found himself gently escorted away from the enthralling table by a graceful lady. She led him to a separate table where his parents awaited. Paul settled into his seat, an intrigued silence enveloping him.

The four enigmatic men at the previous table rose to their feet, raising their glasses in a solemn toast before partaking in the contents. Paul instinctively reached for the drink before him, only to be halted by his mother, who restrained his hand with a subtle shake of her head. Perplexed but obedient, he withdrew his hand.

As the four men began to speak, each taking their turn in the conversation, Paul couldn't help but feel a sense of elusiveness surrounding their words. He strained to grasp their narratives, catching snippets of enthralling stories before they slipped through his fingers.

Upon their conclusion, the men once again raised their glasses in unison, took a sip, and resumed their seats. The remainder of the party followed suit, savoring their drinks with newfound enthusiasm. Paul's mother gave him an acknowledging nod, signaling that he could now partake. He reached for his glass and took a hearty swig, returning to the festivities with the same vigor.

His mother expressed regret, "I am so sorry, Paul. I should have informed you about the party. It was a significant oversight."

Paul offered a reassuring smile, "No problem, Mom. It's been a great time, actually."

"That's good to hear. Did you enjoy our special guests?" she inquired.

Paul smiled and replied, "Yes, I did. But who are they?"

His mother turned to his father, who wore a knowing grin. "You'll find out later, son. Trust me," his father assured.

With a nod, Paul decided to take a leisurely stroll through the gathering, engaging in conversations with various family members who were all relishing the festivities. But the absence of his father's mention of the guests' identities gnawed at him. Paul couldn't shake his curiosity.

Two of the enigmatic men from the head table appeared beside him. "Hey, Paul, remember us?" they asked, their eyes dancing with mischief and power.

"Of course," Paul replied, his curiosity piqued. The one who introduced himself as Dave gestured to his companion, Roger, apologizing for the earlier omission. "Come with us to meet William and Jack. Your mother and father are on their way as well. Follow us," they urged, and Paul, shrugging nonchalantly, decided to comply.

As he followed Dave and Roger, a peculiar realization struck him: he was venturing into a part of the estate he had never before explored. This baffled him, as he had spent his entire childhood and teenage years in this very place. The mystery only deepened as they journeyed deeper into uncharted territory, the surroundings growing ever more bizarre and enigmatic.

Their path led them through a bizarre tunnel, and upon emerging on the other side, Paul was greeted by an astonishing sight. It was as if a colossal wall of monstrous trees had merged to form imposing arches that converged into a grand dome. The leaves, a mesmerizing blend of pink and deep red, hung above them, not a single one touching the ground. Underfoot, a vast expanse of flat stone bore intricate markings that piqued Paul's curiosity. He attempted to decipher them, but their meaning remained elusive.

Drawn to the center of the stone, Paul watched as it rumbled to life, moving beneath his feet moving farther and farther down. He glanced at his mother, whose radiant smile seemed to reflect an inner excitement. The massive stone came to an eventual halt, and everyone disembarked. Before them lay a stunning shoreline, crystal waters, and a colossal ship, a vessel like none Paul had ever seen. Behind it, a mysterious crevice emitted a constant shimmer. Paul couldn't believe his eyes, struggling to comprehend the surreal landscape that surrounded him. It was as though he alone stood in awe, oblivious to the wonders that unfolded before him.

Shaking his head to clear his thoughts, Paul quickened his pace to catch up with the group. They were now walking along a lengthy board leading to the ship. As he moved forward, he couldn't help but marvel at the ship's design, its contours, and features hinting at a world far beyond his previous understanding.

The ship's construction remained an enigma to Paul, defying categorization as wood or metal. Its surface held a strange and elusive shimmer, revealing faint inscriptions within the glistening patterns that resembled liquid script. Paul's gaze became ensnared by the ethereal display, his senses captivated by the ship's otherworldly qualities.

Upon traversing the plank and setting foot on the ship, Paul's amazement did not diminish. Every aspect of this vessel defied the norms of any ship he had ever encountered. It bore a helm and sails, but its design departed from any familiar maritime conventions. Even the deck underfoot felt peculiar, confounding his senses. While he felt anchored to the ground, his movements remained unimpeded, devoid of any sluggishness.

Dave beckoned them to follow, guiding the group to the forecastle. He opened the door and held it ajar, inviting them all inside. "Please, have a seat," Dave offered.

Paul complied, but his curiosity continued to roam freely. His gaze was drawn upward to the upper shelves near the lofty ceiling, where curious giant heads were perched. Their purpose eluded him, and he speculated they might be props of some sort.

Before he could delve deeper into his explorations, Dave addressed him, inquiring about his impressions of the ship. Paul's response was an enthusiastic outpouring of amazement and a flood of questions. Dave, however, suggested that the answers might not hold the same significance that Paul envisioned.

Dave then posed an unexpected question, "How old do you think I am, Paul?"

Paul ventured a guess, "42." His answer prompted Dave and the others to burst into laughter.

But Dave wasn't finished. "What if I told you I am 900 years old, would you believe me?"

Paul chuckled at the incredulity of the notion. "Of course not."

The final revelation left Paul incredulous. "Would you believe that your parents and all the others at this table are the same age as me?" Dave inquired.

Paul's laughter, boisterous and incredulous, echoed through the room. It was laughter that bordered on the absurd, considering the outrageous claim that had been presented to him. Yet, as he gradually composed himself, he realized that he was the sole participant in this laughter. His mirth seemed to hang in the air, unshared, a stark contrast to the somber atmosphere that now enveloped the group. Paul, recognizing his lapse in decorum, offered an apology, "I am sorry for that."

A silent exchange of glances transpired between Paul's parents and Dave, culminating in a subtle nod from the enigmatic figure. Dave spoke, declaring, "Alright, we're done here. We're pleased that you like the ship." The group began to rise from their seats, leaving Paul bewildered, as he questioned whether he had committed some undisclosed offense.

But Paul wasn't ready to let the matter rest. "Hold on a second," he interjected, his curiosity undiminished. "Did you bring me here just to tell me that? You haven't shown me the ship yet, so that can't be the only reason. Okay, I'm listening."

Dave's gaze shifted to Paul's parents, who resumed their seats, followed by the rest of the group. With a measured tone, Dave continued, "Paul, we need to ask you one more question: What have you been working on in your time? Your father has told us that maybe you were onto something."

Paul was taken aback, surprised by the unexpected line of inquiry. Yet, he complied, recounting his private work in detail. With each question they posed, he eagerly provided answers, relishing the opportunity to engage in this intellectually stimulating discussion. The exchange sharpened his mind and elevated his sense of purpose.

Dave then transitioned to the crux of the matter. "So, all in all, what do you think of all you have been studying? Do you believe it could be a real thing, or do you consider it merely myths and legends?"

Paul, considering the question, replied, "Well, of course, I think they are myths, much like Greek myths. But these seem to be obscure and fragmentally hidden all over."

Dave probed further, "But you have compiled these fragments?"

Paul nodded, "Yes, for the most part. There might be missing parts, but how would I know?"

"Now is where we get to the true purpose of this small gathering," Dave declared. "Paul, do you know anything about your ancestors?"

Paul's response was measured, "I do know some things, and what I do know is certainly intriguing. But even with the knowledge I have, there are gaps. My father doesn't seem to have much information about them and rarely discusses it."

Dave leaned forward, his demeanor becoming more solemn. "Well, if I may, I'd like to enlighten you a little."

Dave embarked on a narrative that left Paul awestruck, his storytelling painting vivid images that transported Paul to another world. The details were so immersive that it felt as though he were there in person, witnessing the events unfold. As Dave's tale neared its conclusion, Paul could hardly contain his amazement.

When the story concluded, Paul was left speechless. "That was amazing," he exclaimed. "Honestly, I'm surprised at how closely your story aligns with what I've been studying. Most of the things you mentioned were missing from my research; I had been keeping it concise."

An abrupt bang on the table disrupted the moment. Paul's mother's frustration was palpable as she raised her concerns. "Dammit, son, can we trust you, or should we leave now? We don't have time for this, Dave."

Paul, taken aback by his mother's uncharacteristic anger, looked around the table and responded resolutely, "You can trust me."

With this assurance, Paul's mother settled back into her chair, and Dave continued with the story. "Here is where the story takes a turn," he began. "A little less than three hundred years ago, we were caught off guard, and some of our own lost their lives. Not only that but the very weapons we wielded and the key to the domain of the gods were lost in that fateful event."

Dave leaned in, addressing Paul directly. "Now, young Paul, when we were cosmic travelers, we gathered enough of what you might call an elixir for a moment like this. You see, Paul, we can only ingest a single drop, and that drop grants 300 years of vigorous life. No sickness, no injuries, incredible strength, and an enhanced capacity to endure. This allowed us to acquire even more of the elixir."

However, a somber tone crept into Dave's voice as he continued. "Our forebearer was overzealous. He was aware of the consequences but believed he had built a tolerance over time. He was wrong. His body ascended, with flesh flaking and floating away until he turned to ash, raining down upon us. It was a painful lesson."

Dave's recounting of the past took a darker turn. "Subsequently, we made the mistake of sharing the elixir with our family members once they reached the age of 50. If they were infertile, they remained so, unable to have children. But if they were fertile, they could have as many children as they wished. Many among us seemed to be fertile, and we bestowed this gift on all who reached that age."

Dave's revelations continued, shedding light on a decision that had led to unforeseen consequences. "We had only six originals: me, Roger, William, Jack, your father, and our forebearer. But at one point, we chose to share the elixir with our extended family. Now, as of this night, we have depleted our stores, and only the elders have imbibed it. You, too, shall partake in these final drops to seal our covenant," Dave explained.

Paul, perplexed by the mention of a covenant, leaned back in his chair and asked, "Covenant? What do you mean by that?"

Dave chuckled, his eyes gleaming with an otherworldly certainty. "You will become one of us, joining our mission to retrieve our lost weapons and the key, just as we did almost a millennia ago."

Paul's skepticism was palpable as he challenged, "But you know there are no gods, and there is no way to reach them, even if they did exist."

In response, Jack rose abruptly, seizing a sword from the wall. With a swift motion, he struck Dave in the head with the blade. Paul braced himself, expecting to witness Dave's head roll off, but to his astonishment, Dave's laughter rang out joyously. The bizarre scenario only intensified as Jack turned and forcefully drove the blade into Roger's throat. Roger, too, responded with laughter, and there was not a trace of injury on either of them.

Paul was left in a state of incredulity. His parents, too, joined in the laughter. Was everyone in the room teetering on the brink of madness?

Paul couldn't bear the surreal scene any longer. He grabbed the sword from Jack's hand and exited the cabin. At the helm, he examined the blade, inadvertently slicing his finger. A drop of blood fell onto the deck, and in that moment, his perception shifted. A cosmic battle unfolded before his eyes, featuring a colossal ship and a titanic being locked in fierce combat. The vision was as vivid as it was fleeting. Paul shook his head, baffled by the experience.

As he mulled over the cryptic events and what he had gleaned from his studies, Paul recognized a need to at least play along and appease his parents. After all, what harm could it possibly do?

With newfound determination, Paul returned to the cabin. "I'm in. Let's drink up," he declared. The room erupted with joy, and William poured and distributed the drinks. Dave raised his glass, offering a toast, "To your health and to the covenant we make with you here and now."

As Dave concluded his words, everyone raised their glasses and sipped from them, Paul included. The moment the final drop touched his tongue, an otherworldly transformation overcame him. The room seemed to distort, and the sounds became muffled, like the distant echoes of a dream. It was as if he had plunged into an underwater realm, struggling to breathe, his heart racing relentlessly, and then, an eerie stillness overcame him. The world turned silent, and he felt as though he were peering through a glass submerged in water.

In a heartbeat, his senses returned, and his heart resumed its rhythmic beat. Paul felt electrified, an indescribable surge of energy coursing through him. "You are with us now, one of us," Dave declared. "Let's set forth on our quest and find what we need."

Paul reached for his phone, a repository of the countless fragments, manuscripts, and images from archaeological dig sites he had received from Jeremy. Displaying the evidence to the others, they delved into the discussion. Jack and Roger shared recollections of a particular cave. "I remember this cave," Jack remarked, his words echoed by Roger. Dave affirmed their memories, recalling the fateful ambush that led to their disarming and the theft of the key, nearly sealing their fate in an alien world. "It was a long time ago," Roger reminisced.

Paul, poring over the information, was cautious but forthcoming. "According to what I see here, and with the limited understanding I have, it seems the weapons are located at the bottom, within a mountain, submerged in a lake of fire."

Dave, Roger, Jack, and William exchanged knowing glances, their collective memories returning to a place they were all too familiar with. Jack voiced the concern: "How will we get there, and how do we get past them without our weapons, sir?"

Dave's gaze bore into Jack, and silence settled over the room. Eventually, Dave broke the stillness. "Let's hear what else Paul has to say. Go ahead, Paul, think aloud, and we will listen."

Paul continued, his uncertainty evident. "I'm not sure if this is a key or not, but it seems to be in a place hidden from the eyes of man, beyond human sensation. It's a paradox, something I can't fully grasp."

Dave sighed, and his expression turned somber. "We understand, and it's not in our favor. Both tasks are arduous, but at least we have a direction now—a beacon in the darkness, something we've lacked for far too long."

"Paul, we need more," Dave interjected, his tone tinged with urgency. "You speak of these places that exist yet do not. Without the key, we cannot access them to retrieve our weapons. We must find another means of entry."

Paul furrowed his brow, perplexed. "Entry into where?" he inquired.

"There's an Ethereal Realm, a space between worlds. That mountain you mentioned—it exists there. However, the key's precise location within that realm remains elusive. It's an enigmatic place, vastly different from here," Dave explained.

"So, we need to find a way into this ethereal realm?" Paul sought confirmation.

"Yes," Dave affirmed. "It could involve star alignment rituals, peculiar occurrences, or anything that seems out of the ordinary to you."

Frustration etched Paul's features as he pored over his phone. "This feels too limited. I need to return to my house," he declared.

"Let's go then," Dave agreed. They all rose, retracing their steps. As they walked, Paul marveled at the unfolding events. Upon arriving at his house, he offered them drinks before diving into his work. Dave and Jack joined in, poring over the material spread across Paul's desk. Time slipped away unnoticed.

Suddenly, Paul's phone chimed. "Who would message me at this time?" he wondered aloud, reaching for his device. It was Jeremy, sharing more pictures and his insights on their potential significance. Paul immersed himself in the content, then turned to Dave with newfound determination. "I've found the mountain we need to reach. But I thought you said it existed in another plane," Paul questioned.

Dave's smile held a hint of mystery. "Yes, the mountain itself exists in this plane. However, the river of fire and the guardians—their realm is separate. You'll understand when we get there."

"Sir, we still don't know how to get in," Jack voiced his concern.

"I know," Dave responded, his tone brimming with determination.

"Hold on, hold on," Paul interrupted, excitement glinting in his eyes. "Jeremy says it looks like the blood of what he understands to be a Molkien—whatever that is—on the three pillars of beyond sight could open our eyes to the real world, or something like that. His interpretation might be off, though," Paul relayed.

"There it is!" Dave exclaimed. "Boys, let's go."

"Now? It's the middle of the night. Why not wait until morning?" Paul implored.

Laughter filled the room. "You don't need to sleep, my friend. I mean, you can, but there's no need," Roger reassured him.

William, who seldom spoke, suddenly chimed in, "We should leave him here anyway, don't you think, Dave?"

Dave turned to Paul. "You're one of us now. You have to learn what we do. We are not only men of letters, son; we are ancient warriors. It's a task we've undertaken for centuries. Lately, we've been inactive, but we've been training. Life is the best teacher," Dave explained firmly.

"He'll come with us," William, Roger, and Jack affirmed in unison. Paul's mother expressed her unease, but after a reassuring glance from Paul's father, she reluctantly agreed.

Paul was left speechless but decided to play along. "So where are we going?" Dave inquired.

"We're headed for Tibet," Paul declared, a smile lighting up his face. Paul's father swiftly arranged their plane tickets and called for a cab. The pace was rapid; there was no room for delay. "Men of action, I guess," Paul mused, feeling both nervous and excited, completely unsure of what lay ahead.

Paul messaged Jeremy about his imminent trip to the place mentioned in his recent message. As the cab arrived and they all prepared to leave, Jeremy's call came through. "Paul, don't—" The line crackled, "—bad." Then, abruptly, the call dropped.

Amidst the hustle, Jeremy's call got brushed off, fading from Paul's mind almost as soon as it was cut off. He deemed it normal, nothing significant. They swiftly reached the airport, boarded their plane, and the flight seemed to breeze by. Landing in Ngari, they secured a hotel and engaged in some conversation. "What now?" Paul queried. Dave chuckled, "Go to the mountain, of course," he stated. Paul's father had already left to arrange a car. Upon his return, an electric energy buzzed through the air, palpable excitement coursed through everyone. But Paul sensed an underlying tension, an unusual vibe that made him uneasy. These people were intense, and if they were anxious about something, it had to be serious, he pondered.

As they drove, an eerie silence enveloped the car. Lost in their thoughts, their eyes stared into the void. Paul began feeling a twinge of worry. The extended period of inactivity seemed to have made them nervous, heightening his concern about the reality of this mission.

Parking the car behind a dense bush, Paul's father declared, "We walk from here." Exiting the vehicle, they commenced the ascent up the mountain, a journey that unfolded in complete silence. Then, abruptly, Dave halted. "There it is." Paul only discerned a shadow on the rock; what Dave saw was beyond his perception. Roger, seemingly nonchalant, approached the shadow, slashed his palm with a dagger, and smeared a blood arc on the shadowed rock. As he stepped back, an astonishing sight unfolded—what appeared to be a cave emerged from the shadow. Paul couldn't believe his eyes. "Come," Dave beckoned, and without a word, he ventured into the cave.

Paul turned to Roger, his curiosity piqued. "How did you know to do that?" he asked. Roger shrugged. "I didn't. I just thought if our blood opened the veil, it might work here too," he replied. "But how did you guys even know that could be a doorway inside?" Paul pressed, bewildered. "That comes with experience in these things. Many occurrences you perceive as normal or strange often hold deeper significance," Roger explained.

As they navigated the tunnels, the rocky surroundings faded, replaced by a labyrinthine cave system. Dave and the others were already ahead, prompting Roger and Paul to hasten their pace. Paul found himself leading, guided by what he believed was a map to the three pillars. Unsettled by the unknown, he drew comfort from the readiness of the group. The four men exuded strength and athleticism, their fiery-eyed demeanor contrasting sharply with Paul's perception of his own parents as normal, albeit exceptionally healthy, individuals.

They turned a corner and entered a larger, open area with towering 50-foot pillars, not made of rock but living structures. Paul was awestruck. "What are these? They look alive," he inquired. "These are the living pillars of Neverlasting," Dave replied.

Curiosity lingered in Paul's voice. "Now what?" Roger, William, and Jack approached the pillars, but as they were about to cut their hands, the ground violently shook. Guardians, majestic yet formidable creatures, emerged from concealed alcoves and passages within the cavern walls, their metallic bodies gleaming in the cave's dim illumination.

The metallic clinks and the crackling flames adorned their armor, creating an otherworldly symphony of sound. Towering guardians stood before them, their forms etched with intricate designs and blazing runes, exuding an intense, fiery energy. "Molkiens, you shall not pass," the six guardians proclaimed in unison.

Suddenly, Dave surged forward, appearing larger and more formidable than ever. "And who shall stop us?" he boldly challenged. But before the echoes of his words faded, the guardians lunged at him. "Hurry, open the gate!" Dave shouted to the others by the pillars. However, all 6 of the guardians redirected their course toward them, threatening to intercept their attempt.

In a blur of motion, Dave leaped, taking down two colossal beasts with a thunderous crash. Paul's father charged forward, a towering figure of strength and ferocity, crashing into two more guardians with unbridled force. It was a side of his father Paul had never witnessed.

Despite the efforts of the men, two guardians remained on course, closing in on at least two of the three pillars. Yet, by now, all three men had slashed their hands and placed them within the pillars. Fire and lightning surged around them, freezing the guardians in their tracks, while Dave and Paul's father fought fiercely against the rest.

Then, a sonic boom shattered the reality around them, revealing a strange, dark, and twisted place. Paul couldn't believe his eyes—everything was real. Amidst the pillars, a colossal circle of molten rock and fire pulsated, marking where the weapons lay—searing lines of fire carved through the solid rock, tracing a scorching path toward each guardian. As the flames made contact, they danced across the etched curves and markings on the metallic forms, turning the metal into a fiery orange hue while the rest of their bodies glowed an eerie blue. Wicked, twisted grins stretched across the intense faces of the guardians, sending shivers down Paul's spine.

"Dad!" Paul cried out as Dave, William, Roger, and Jack called out to his father, Carter. With a glance at Paul, his father turned towards the pool of fire. His skin morphed, taking on stone-like scales as his stature expanded, and with determination, he dove into the fiery pool. Two of the guardians followed him in, while Dave, Jack, and William engaged the remaining foes.

Paul stood frozen, disbelief etched on his face. Suddenly, something shot out of the fiery pool, landing with a resounding clang beside him. It resembled a massive Zande, a weapon of some sort. "Pick it up, Paul, and strike them down!" Dave's urgent command pierced through the chaos. Without hesitation, Paul stooped and grabbed the Zande. As his fingers closed around it, the weapon began to glow with a pulsating blue light, quivering in his grasp. The vibrations resonated through his body, triggering an electrifying surge of adrenaline.

Paul sprang to life, dashing toward Dave and the engaged guardian. With a decisive swing, he severed its head, then turned to Roger, thrusting the Zande into the guardian he was battling. The other two guardians, now focused on Paul, menacingly approached. Before they could reach him, a figure leaped out of the fiery pit, tearing the guardians apart. In stunned silence, Paul dropped the Zande. It was his father, now standing in human form.

Speechless, Paul watched as Carter handed each of the men their weapons. "Here you go, boys, we got 'em. That wasn't so bad, right?" Carter jested. Dave and the rest smiled in agreement. "We got them. It sure feels good to hold these again," Roger remarked, and the rest shared the sentiment. Finally shaking off the shock, Paul asked, "What's next?"

Dave laughed, "Look around you, Paul. Does this look like the place we came into?" Paul, realizing the surroundings were vastly different from their entry point, asked, "Where are we?" William replied, "In the place you can't see or feel."

"Okay, let's go," Dave said, starting to walk, with the others following. "We have a search before us, Paul. The key is here, but where is the question. We really do not want to draw attention to ourselves; there are things here that do not like our kind, especially when we enter their domains," Dave cautioned.

Jack interjected, "You know that's impossible here, though. Come on, Dave." Dave chuckled, "We can try," he said. Jack shrugged. This world was strange, and Paul struggled to find words to describe his thoughts—it was pure wonderment, a mind paralyzed by the inexplicable. Laws of physics didn't seem to apply here, or at least not the same way he was used to. While the rest seemed unfazed, even his father appeared normal. Despite the fear, Paul followed, trusting they knew what they were doing, although he was far from comfortable.

They navigated through bizarre orientations—upside down, sideways, even through solid objects—sending shivers down Paul's spine. Eventually, they arrived at a colossal expanse, a vast void with floating and shifting land masses. "Well, boys, it looks like we have no choice but to get seen," Dave declared.

Without hesitation, Dave leaped into the air, the others following suit. Paul's father, turning to him, offered reassurance, "Just trust it, Paul. Things are different here." With that, he jumped, leaving Paul anxious and searching for an alternative route. Finding none, he reluctantly dove off the edge, plummeting downward. As he fell, a massive tentacle seized him, bringing him to the creature it belonged to.

Now standing before an indescribable being, Paul was paralyzed by fear. The creature took a deep breath before speaking. "The way you seek the key is dangerous. We all know you are here; your flesh cries out in this place. I will help you on one condition: when you and the Molkiens ravage the domains of the gods, vow to spare me and my domains," it proposed.

Paul, unsure of the rules but aware of his companions' fervor for the key, agreed, "I don't know the rules, but I'm sure Dave and the rest would be pleased about this. They want that key badly."

The creature accepted his agreement. A drop of Paul's blood hovered in the air, moving toward the creature's outstretched palm. It nestled into the creature's hand, transforming into a red crystal. In an instant, Paul vanished. Darkness surrounded him, and echoing words filled his mind: "Alzor, the red dragon Inn table 8." When sight returned, he found himself back in the hotel room.

Pouring a drink, Paul sat down and grabbed a pen and paper from his desk. He wrote down the words "Alzor, the red dragon Inn table 8" and sat back, contemplating, as he sipped his drink.

Within minutes, the door burst open with life as Dave, Jack, William, Roger, and Paul's father flooded into the room. "There you are. What happened to you?" his father inquired. Paul recounted the encounter, showing them the note. A strange tension filled the air, and Paul couldn't shake the feeling that he might have done something wrong. "Did I do something wrong?" he asked. "I thought you'd be happy; we can get the key," he insisted.

"You've put us in debt to Alzor, which is not a good place," Dave responded sternly. Despite Paul's optimism about obtaining the key, Dave and the others exchanged disapproving glances. "You know something is not right; it's Alzor. Come on," Roger chimed in.

The door opened again, and Paul's mother entered the room, declaring, "We go to the Red Dragon." All other conversations ceased, and the group concurred. Paul wondered how his mother had known where to go, but shrugged it off. After a quick round of eating, showering, and preparations, they headed to the inn. The establishment featured a spacious lounge area where they secured a booth and ordered drinks.

Feeling a bit left out and wanting something more, Paul walked up to the bar. The bartender promptly attended to him, and as Paul ordered and sat on the adjacent stool, he indulged in a couple of drinks. A voice from his right interrupted his thoughts. "Rough day, buddy?" the voice inquired.

Turning to face the speaker, Paul found a sharp-eyed, hard-faced, clean-shaven older gentleman, impeccably dressed and exuding the scent of myrrh. "You could say that," Paul replied, taking another sip. The older man smiled, exchanged a nod with the bartender, and suggested, "I think I might have something to help you with that." Paul smiled back, nodding as the bartender placed a crimson drink in front of him. "Drink," the older gentleman instructed.

With hesitation, Paul grasped the glass and took a sip. As the liquid touched his lips, he could have sworn that the old man's eyes sparked a fleeting flash of green, though uncertainty clouded his observation. The drink itself was a delightful blend of sweetness and bitterness, a peculiar harmony that somehow suited the moment.

"Once you're done with your drink, you should feel better and see better," the old man remarked. Paul had intended to savor the beverage, but it vanished before he realized it. A warm glow permeated his body and mind, and his vision shimmered, revealing a new layer to the world around him. Despite the strangeness of the room, his attention was captivated by the massive golden doors.

The older man smiled approvingly, "Good, you can see now. Yes, go through that door." However, when Paul turned back to ask questions, the old man had disappeared. Puzzled, he queried the bartender, "Where is the older gentleman that was here with me?"

The bartender appeared confused, "Sorry, sir, I haven't seen anyone in that chair for a while now." Paul gestured towards the glass that should have been in front of the older man, but only his own glass remained. Undeterred, he looked for the golden doors and found them still visible.

Returning to the booth where the others sat, Paul reassured them, "I'm okay, just follow me." Despite their confusion, they followed him as he walked toward the doors. However, the doors seemed farther than they appeared earlier. Upon reaching them, Paul grabbed the knobs, and as he swung the door open, the others could now see the seemingly empty void before them.

"How did you know?" Paul's father inquired. "Tell you later. Let's go," Paul replied, and without further explanation, they all jumped into the unknown.

Emerging on the other side, they found themselves in yet another dimension. Paul couldn't help but notice that each of them now possessed weapons. "Hey, where did those come from?" Paul inquired.

"They have been on us the whole time, on the physical plane they can't be seen," Roger explained. Paul, still trying to process the unfolding mysteries, questioned, "Now what?"

A sinister laughter echoed through the air. "Step forward, Molkiens," a voice thundered through the mist. As they cautiously moved forward, the mist lifted, revealing an enigmatic figure in a deep red cloak hovering before them.

"Ah, the Molkiens, the bastard children of Saphirnil," the figure declared. He continued, recounting the betrayal of Saphirnil and the demise of the mighty god. "I am the sacred Guardian, and none shall pass," he proclaimed. Expressing surprise at their discovery of the place, he laughed menacingly and pointed at Paul. "Hahaha, I can smell Alzor on you, boy."

Dave and the others drew their weapons, advancing towards the Sacred Guardian. The ground shook, and a beastly figure emerged, standing between them and their target. Without hesitation, they attacked, but their weapons seemed ineffective against the formidable foe. As they struggled in combat, Paul's mother calmly walked past the fray, heading directly for the Sacred Guardian. Standing before him, the power emanating from the Guardian blew back her hair and clothes. In a soft and composed voice, she spoke, but the Guardian couldn't hear her well.

"Speak up, woman! I cannot hear your words," he demanded with authority. She looked up and gestured for him to come closer so she could convey her message.

Approaching until she could feel the heat of his breath, tainted by the stench of death, Paul's mother waited for the right moment. In a soft, almost inaudible whisper, she spoke, her hand emerging from under her shawl. Swiftly, she drove a massive spike through the bottom of the Sacred Guardian's jaw, up through the top of his head, and through the folds of his red cloak. The man-beast turned to dust, and the Sacred Guardian wailed and cursed as Paul's mother, unfazed, grabbed Paul's father's weapon, severing the head cleanly. An emerald key fell to the ground, and she knelt to pick it up.

A profound silence enveloped them for a few seconds until Dave broke it. "Okay, let's go," he said. Paul, still processing the surreal events, questioned, "Okay, how?" His mother smiled, holding the key as if unlocking an invisible door. The others gathered around her, and Paul followed suit. With a turn of the key, they found themselves back in their hotel room. Though Paul was astonished, he kept his thoughts to himself, not wanting to appear childish.

Amidst the amazement, Paul's phone buzzed with a barrage of notifications from Jeremy. Before he could check the messages, the group prepared to depart, taking an alternate route. They stood around Paul's mother once again, and as she turned the key, they materialized in the courtyard of Paul's parents' house.

Just as Dave was about to speak, Paul's mother intervened, suggesting that Paul had experienced enough for the night and they might continue in the morning. The others exchanged irritated glances, but Paul's father gave a subtle nod, prompting her to move aside for a private conversation. Meanwhile, Paul went to check his phone, and Jack, placing a hand on his shoulder, teased, "Hey, what are you doing, buddy? Talking to the ladies?"

"No, no, my friend Jeremy has been trying to get a hold of me, and it looks like it could be important," Paul replied. Jack acknowledged with an understanding nod. Soon after, Roger approached Paul, giving a friendly pat on the same shoulder that held the phone. In an unfortunate turn of events, Paul dropped it, and it shattered upon impact. Instantly, he sank to the ground, devastated by the loss. Though he recognized the irrationality of his distress, the weight of losing everything on the phone overwhelmed him momentarily.

Just as Paul grappled with his emotions, his parents returned. "I spoke too soon; it would be best to get as much done as soon as possible," his mother declared. Looking up from the ground, Paul felt a mix of confusion and frustration. He questioned the urgency, suggesting they had 300 years before any further actions were needed. However, his mother's response was unexpected. "Do you understand anything? Are you so grounded in nonsense?" she yelled. Witnessing his mom losing her temper and raising her voice again, Paul realized this situation must be serious.

Resigned, Paul agreed to go with the rest of the group. Handing the broken phone to his mother, he thanked her, and she assured him that she would take care of it. As she left for the house, Paul's father, Carter, cast an intense gaze at the men. Paul, witnessing yet another unexpected behavior from his father, felt a growing sense of unease. With a wild look in his eyes, Carter rallied the group. "Let us shake off the rust, boys!" he cheered, leading them to the secret place they had visited earlier. Paul's unease deepened as he observed the others, equally wild-eyed, following his father.

They approached the remarkable ship they had boarded before, but this time, they walked past it, heading toward the peculiar shimmer that beckoned them forward.

Dave issued instructions to the group as they gathered near the shimmering gateway. "I will open the gates, you know what to do. Show Paul his task, yell when all is ready," he directed. Carter and the others nodded in understanding, boarding the ship as Paul followed suit. Jack pulled Paul aside, emphasizing the importance of his task. "Stick to it until we are stable," Jack instructed, and Paul, determined, nodded in agreement.

From his position, Paul's father shouted, and Dave responded, inserting the key into the slot. The shimmer swelled and heaved, prompting Dave to sprint back to the ship. Seizing the plank, he pulled it onto the vessel. Suddenly, Paul felt the ship bobbing, and Roger swiftly moved around, cutting the anchoring ropes. Then, a breathtaking sight unfolded before Paul – a colossal wave of galaxies surged and swirled. Mesmerized, he watched as each man, abandoning their posts, hung over the ship's sides, striking their weapons against the ethereal waves. The resulting spray clung to them like mystical armor, leaving Paul in awe.

Carter approached Paul, handing him a weapon. "Take this and strike the waves. This is your weapon from now on," he explained. The other men looked at Carter with disdain, realizing that he would now have to go without a weapon. While they understood, it still raised concerns. "Quick, we don't have much time. The reservoir is almost ready. Hurry!" Carter urged. Paul, now armed with his father's weapon, sliced through the ethereal waves, feeling an electric charge as the spray enveloped him. His father shouted, "Get to your post, hurry!" Paul rushed to his position just as an incredible popping sound echoed through the surroundings. In an instant, they were no longer in the underground caverns but adrift in the vastness of the cosmos that had been pouring in. Paul's mind reeled – how was he breathing? Was he breathing at all? The mysteries of this new dimension engulfed him.

He surveyed the crew, and each member seemed more animated than the living, a blazing fire evident in their eyes. Paul wondered if his eyes mirrored the same intensity. The ship had achieved stability, sailing smoothly with only Dave at the helm, steering the magical vessel with effortless mastery. Paul's father and the others joined him, acknowledging his efforts.

"You can relax now, Dave has it. Good job," Paul's father commended. The crew gathered around Paul, and William issued instructions. "For the first capture, we want you to watch over the whole process. Don't overreact; it will be a problem. We will yell if there is something specific we need. Other than that, just watch and do not panic, okay?" William said, fixing his gaze on Paul. Paul nodded in agreement. "Yeah, okay," he replied.

"Perhaps you should take the weapon, Carter," Roger suggested, earning a stern look from Carter. "Sorry," Roger quickly added. From the helm, Dave yelled, "Get ready." The crew descended into the ship's depths, retrieving monstrous chains and massive objects unfamiliar to Paul. William and Roger handled an enormous piece resembling a narwhal horn but far larger. They screwed it into the ship's bow, causing it to extend prominently. As it cut through the ethereal, it changed color and glowed. Four more massive pieces, rising above the masts, were secured into the deck. Massive chains and shackles were bolted to three of them, then looped through the fourth central one. Paul marveled at their strength and wondered if he, too, possessed such power.

Dave's voice bellowed, "Shall we start where we left off?" The crew cheered in response, and with a resolute nod, he spun the wheel, causing the ship to reel around.

From a silver chest, William extracted a peculiar instrument, placing it carefully on the table before him. He then drew his weapon, pricked his finger, and let a drop of blood fall onto one of the six gemstones embedded in the instrument. A powerful beam shot into the ethereal, crashing onto the massive horn at the ship's bow. A surge of energy cascaded over the vessel, and Dave relinquished control of the helm as the ship began steering itself. Racing at incredible speed, the ship charged toward an unknown destination, the ethereal seemingly thickening and becoming denser, making it harder for the vessel to cut through.

Paul felt the ethereal against his skin, a constant static sensation, occasionally intensifying to the point where it felt like he might float off the ship. "Paul, get in here!" Jack's urgent voice echoed as he pulled on a latch in the deck. He revealed a shielded hut for Paul to stay in during the capture. Inside the hut, Paul peered through a rectangular slit, witnessing the entire ship coming alive as the crew prepared for the imminent capture. Tension hung in the air, and then it arrived—a monstrous being passed by the ship. The noise was deafening, a chaotic blend of yells and indistinct words, drowning out Paul's thoughts. Yet, he continued to watch as the being passed again, and again.

Unable to get a clear look, Paul sensed its enormity. Then, on the starboard side, he saw it—a god, great and terrible. Paul couldn't believe his eyes. As the god prepared to strike down, the ship spun at the last moment, thrusting the horn into the god's chest. The god struggled, unable to free itself. Roger and William ran along the horn, jumping onto the mighty arms of the god, swiftly securing enormous shackles. They returned to the center pole, spinning it with determined resolve.

The mighty horn retracted into the ship, the chains dragged the god across the deck towards the center. Great chains hoisted it up the pole, and William and Roger swiftly secured chains around the god's thrashing feet. A fierce struggle ensued; sparks danced in the air as the power of the chains clashed with the god's might. Eventually, the chains tightened, rendering the god motionless. Its eyes seethed, emitting fiery sparks. "I smell new flesh, Molkiens," it hissed. "New one, for what purpose do you hunt gods? For a taste of immortality—a small taste, child. You cannot create or deal with the matters of the dead. You'll get a few hundred years, maybe a few thousand, of a pain-free life, a death-free life. And if you're lucky, you might gain an ability you didn't have before," the god laughed.

Paul emerged from behind his shield, ignoring Dave's warnings to stay back. "Is this an evil god, like you said?" Paul inquired. "Yes, he is one of the worst," Dave confirmed. "He will say anything to trick you into thinking we're doing something wrong. But why not rid the cosmos of tainted gods and reap the rewards?" Dave questioned. Encouraged by Dave's words, Paul stepped forward toward the chained god. The god seethed with smoke, fire, and power. "Please tell me, explain," Paul requested. Before the god could respond, the massive narwhal horn, which had retracted from the front, emerged through a hole in the deck. It pierced the god from under its jaw, through the top of its head, and then the deck dropped out from under it, sending it into the bowels of the ship.

LEGENDS OF THE UNSEEN

The deck closed up, leaving only the tip of the horn protruding. An odd color of ethereal mist lingered around the tip, growing by the second. William rushed to grab an object resembling an ancient gold urn. He positioned himself at the tip, patiently waiting until the mist had grown immensely in size, then gently guided it into the urn. The men erupted in cheers and joyous celebration. "Men," Dave exclaimed, "this was an easy one, one of the easiest we have done. Perfect for Paul's first experience!" They cheered again, and Paul's father patted him on the shoulder. "Wild ride, eh?" he said. Paul looked at him, uncertain of what to say. "Ya, it sure was," he replied. His father smiled, "He was only going to lie, son. That's what the ones we hunt do; they don't like people," he explained. Paul wasn't sure; it seemed like they just didn't like Molkiens. He decided to keep an eye out; something felt off.

Upon leaving the ethereal, they didn't return to his parents' house but ended up in a different cave, adorned with numerous artifacts. Overwhelmed with excitement, Paul walked around the cave, inspecting the unique collection. The others tended to the massive god in the ship, allowing Paul to indulge in his fascination. Suddenly, a loud gong echoed, drawing Paul's attention to two massive amethyst doors beginning to open. They guided the god on a massive floating cart into the doors, and Paul followed them in, eager to witness the unfolding events. Inside, his mind struggled to comprehend the wonders, but the center stage featured an enormous tear-dropped glass structure. The god was brought there, and Roger, climbing onto the cart, raised it to the top, approximately 20 feet high. At the summit, Roger performed strange gestures, causing the god to float over the narrow opening of the massive tear-drop glass, where a stream of what looked like galaxies rapidly poured into it.

The enormous glass quickly approached fullness, halting abruptly, causing the god's lifeless carcass to collapse back onto the cart. Roger rode the cart down to the ground, and whispered something to Dave. Paul strained to hear their conversation, but their eyes were fixed on the god's remains. Suddenly, without warning, the god's limp body erupted into a chaotic explosion, releasing dark creatures that scattered in all directions. Paul's father shouted, realizing that the god wasn't a god at all; it was a decoy, a vessel for the dark entities they had unwittingly unleashed.

Before another word could be uttered, the creatures swarmed them. Some flew, while others moved like shadows on the ground, their speed and agility making them difficult to track. Paul found himself surrounded, witnessing flashes of black whizzing past him. His father's voice cut through the chaos, urging him to use his weapon and fight. However, Paul stood transfixed and somewhat shocked. The creatures tore at his flesh, and his father fought fiercely, moving with the agility of a jungle cat, while the others skillfully battled the shadowy masses.

Amid the mayhem, Paul's father clawed his way through the hordes to reach his son. However, when he finally reached the spot where Paul had stood, the dark creatures had completely covered him. Paul's father dove into the pile, tearing them off, only to discover that Paul had vanished. The remaining creatures disappeared, leaving everyone standing there, ready and bewildered. Dave questioned why and who took Paul, but Paul's father could only shake his head. Jake pressed further, asking who knew about them. William didn't mince words, acknowledging that they became a beacon as soon as they started retrieving their items. Roger added, "It has to be Alzor; he made a deal with Paul and, in turn, showed us how to get the key."

"I concur, but how did it manage to escape? We have wards in place, nothing should be able to leave this room," Dave questioned. A realization dawned on the rest.

"Indeed, what about that?" William chimed in. In unison, they began scrutinizing the room's protective measures. After a brief inspection, Paul's father, Carter, made a discovery.

"I believe I've found it. Three of the twelve crystals are out of their slots, and we wouldn't have noticed because they were from the bottom row, concealed behind the casing," he revealed.

"No one but us has access to this place. Someone from our own ranks has betrayed our clan," Dave asserted. Suspicion hung heavily in the air as they all stared at each other, grappling with the unsettling revelation.

The tension in the room was palpable, a heavy silence enveloping them as they each grappled with the unsettling revelation. Finally, Dave broke the silence, his voice weighted with concern.

"All right, we might as well reconvene at Carter's. We need to piece this together before we can move forward," he declared. With unanimous agreement, they made their way to Carter's house.

Upon arrival, they were greeted by Paul's mother, who had prepared a lavish spread of food and drink. Her eyes shone with anticipation, but her excitement turned to despair when she inquired about Paul's whereabouts. Carter's expression darkened as he delivered the grim news.

"They took him. We don't know how, but someone has him. Most likely Alzor," he revealed. The room erupted in chaos for a moment before Paul's mother silenced them with a stern rebuke, her voice carrying a mixture of anger and sorrow.

Once the commotion settled, Carter addressed the room solemnly, revealing the harsh reality of betrayal within their ranks. Though no accusations were made, suspicion lingered heavily among them, casting a pall over the gathering.

As they sat down to eat and drink, consumed by their own thoughts, Paul's mother stood up with a steely resolve, her words cutting through the somber atmosphere.

"Now that you've had your fill, it's time to find my son. And this time, I'm coming with you," she declared. Carter nodded in agreement, and they rose from the table, the weight of their mission hanging heavy upon them.

Meanwhile, Paul found himself in a state of confusion and darkness. One moment he was with his father and the others, the next, they were under attack, and everything went black. Now, he was in a void of darkness, surrounded by an ominous presence and eerie whispers echoing in the abyss.

In the suffocating darkness, a voice sliced through the void, chilling Paul to the bone. "I am delighted that you've graced me with your presence," it hissed. Paul's voice trembled as he responded, "I had no choice. Who are you, and what do you want from me?" The voice boomed with laughter, mocking Paul's audacity. "Who are you to demand answers from me, mortal? Nevertheless, you serve a purpose, insignificant as you may be," it taunted. As the voice drew nearer, the darkness began to recede, revealing a ghastly creature bathed in a dim red glow. Paul's attempt to mask his fear failed miserably. "Ah, it's you," he muttered, trying to conceal his terror. "Your fear is palpable, human," the creature sneered. "What's happening?" Paul stammered. "You have a role to play, my young friend. Our agreement permits me to do as I please," the creature explained. "I didn't agree to this!" Paul protested. The creature's laughter echoed, disdain dripping from its voice. "You humans are so limited in your understanding," it mocked before darkness consumed Paul once more, engulfing him entirely.

Meanwhile, on the deck of the ship, Paul's mother took charge, pushing the men to devise a solution. Frustrated with the lack of progress, she retreated to the cabin, hinting at her own capabilities. As murmurs of confusion and concern rippled among the men, Carter attempted to rationalize her actions. "Perhaps she's acquired a new ability," he suggested. William voiced his unease, questioning her secrecy. Carter's gaze hardened at William's remark, though Jack concurred with the sentiment. "She should have informed us. Transparency is key among us," Jack asserted. Carter reluctantly nodded in agreement, acknowledging the validity of their concerns. Moments later, Paul's mother emerged from the cabin, directing Roger to fetch William's gadget. With all eyes on her, she set to work, her actions cloaked in mystery and intrigue.

Once the instrument was set up, Paul's mother delicately pricked her finger, allowing a single drop of blood to fall onto its pinnacle. In an instant, the device sprang to life, swirling with a fervor that left the men bewildered yet intrigued. As the instrument steadied, the ship surged through the ethereal, guided by the direction indicated by the mystical contraption. Sensing the impending battle, everyone braced themselves for the challenges ahead.

"Where are we headed, my love?" Carter inquired, concern etched into his features.

"We're going after the big fish," she declared, fire leaping from her eyes.

Carter's apprehension surfaced. "But we're short a man. We'll be risking everything," Carter insisted, attempting to dissuade her.

She glared back at him, her eyes flashing with intensity. "Nickel-and-diming power, for how long, Carter? How long?" She shook her head, her resolve evident in her voice. "No, I will endure it no longer," she declared.

Carter's gaze softened as he pleaded, "What about our son? Shouldn't we find him first?"

Ignoring his plea, she turned away, her mind set on her course of action. Meanwhile, Carter approached the others, relaying his wife's plan and the urgency of their preparations. Though none believed it to be a prudent decision, they understood the gravity of their situation and diligently readied themselves, fortifying their defenses and bracing for the impending onslaught.

Summoning Carter once more, Paul's mother conveyed the importance of readiness amidst the fast-approaching events. Carter nodded, his unease palpable as uncertainty loomed over their perilous journey.

These men, veterans in the battle against gods, possessed a fearlessness that surpassed even the bravest mortals. Yet, the god they now approached instilled a deep-seated terror in each of them. He was among the mightiest, a distant deity who cared little for the affairs of the mortal world but wielded unparalleled power. Draining him promised not just longevity, but true immortality—a prize beyond measure. However, the process required precision; an overdose could result in a catastrophic explosion, while too little would yield no more effect than their current situation.

Unlike the gods they had captured before, this one held the potential for absolute immortality with a single dose—an unprecedented feat. As they hurtled toward their target, Paul's mother's eyes blazed with determination. "We're almost there. Ready yourselves, men."

Each crew member assumed their position, preparing for the impending encounter. Amidst the ethereal expanse, magnificent creatures danced and flickered, but the crew remained steadfast, their focus fixed on the looming entity ahead. Before them, a colossal formation resembling an eye pulsated with life, with Paul hovering in front of it.

"It's Paul!" Carter exclaimed, his voice filled with urgency. Paul's mother, her resolve unyielding, halted the ship with a simple gesture. The crew held their breath, poised for action. From the eye, a monstrous hand emerged, reaching hungrily for Paul. With each evasive move, Paul slipped further from its grasp until, with a tremendous effort, the entity tore itself free.

Paul watched in awe as the god, exuding power and malevolence, closed in on him. Paralyzed with fear, he could only await his fate as the god's grin widened with anticipation.

Paul's mother extended her hand, commanding the ship to surge forward toward the god and Paul. Yet, before they reached their target, the god had drained Paul's life force, leaving his limp form suspended in the ethereal void. The ship's horn pierced through the gods chest, and the crew raced along the chains, struggling against the god's immense power to secure them in place. Despite their efforts, the god's strength threatened to pull the ship into the eye.

With frantic determination, the god locked eyes with Paul's mother, fire leaped from them licking toward her. Suddenly, a force from behind cleaved through his torso, altering his expression, before the horn retracted and the chains swiftly dragged him into position. The crew watched in astonishment as Alzor, wielding a colossal golden heart, dispatched the god, he nodded to Paul's mother and disappeared as quickly as he had appeared. Their curiosity piqued, they turned to Paul's mother.

Setting aside their questions for the moment, the crew focused on their task, maneuvering the ship toward the draining den. In tense silence, they executed their duties with precision. As the god's essence poured into the massive glass vessel, Paul's mother observed, as a silent witness to the process unfolding before her.

As the god's form dissipated, a peculiar object resembling a large seed fell into the cosmic liquid within the glass. Bewildered, Dave questioned its nature, but Carter could only offer uncertainty as they approached the vessel. Slowly, the liquid began to swirl and unfurl, revealing a radiant figure bathed in a strange blue aura—Paul, transformed by forces beyond comprehension.

When Paul's mother witnessed the scene unfolding before her, a sting of fear pricked her heart. Paul appeared strangely calm, effortlessly walking through the glass barrier without so much as a crack. His gaze locked onto his mother, prompting her to react swiftly. With urgency, she dashed toward the crystals, kicking one out and slicing her hand upon it. In a desperate move, she pressed her bleeding hand against a blood safety, triggering Paul's instant extraction and immersion into the ethereal realm.

A cry of accusation pierced the air as William's accusation echoed through the chamber. The other men, fueled by anger and confusion, closed in on Paul's mother, demanding answers for her actions. However, before she could respond, a sudden rush of wind swept through the room, accompanied by a tantalizing mist and scent that filled the air with its sweet and spicy aroma. As the mist dissipated, a formidable female figure materialized before them, her presence commanding attention and respect.

The goddess surveyed the men with a penetrating gaze before addressing them with a tone of authority. She chastised the Molkiens for their audacity in seizing what was not rightfully theirs, insinuating that nature or divinity would have bestowed such gifts upon them had they proven worthy. Her words hung heavily in the air.

"Do you know why I am here?" Her voice carried a weight of ages, resonating through the chamber. "I smelled the scent of my companion, with whom I have been since infinity's beginning. But then you Molkiens took him. How, I do not know. But how, then, have I smelled his savory scent?" Her words hung heavy in the air, echoing off the walls of the chamber.

The men exchanged uneasy glances, their eyes flickering with uncertainty, as they turned to Paul's mother. The goddess hovered, an ethereal presence between them, her gaze piercing through the darkness. With a solemn intensity, she locked eyes with Paul's mother and drew in a deep breath through her nose.

"Oh, my dear," her voice carried a mix of sorrow and revelation, "he has been in you." Carter's glare bore into the goddess, his every muscle tensed with defiance, yet her gaze held him at bay. "You must be her mate," she acknowledged.

A smile played on her lips as she turned back to Paul's mother. With a flicker of desperation, Paul's mother raised her hand to gather power, only to find it faltering, slipping through her fingers like sand. The goddess's laughter reverberated through the chamber, a chilling reminder of her dominion over their fate.

"He has betrayed you, mortal," her words cut through the silence like a knife. "Alzor is king now of a new, more powerful domain. You were a pawn." Dread crept across Paul's mother's face. "Oh, fear not, little one," the goddess said with a mix of pity and resolve, as she leaned forward and kissed Paul's mother's forehead. Instantly, she began to disintegrate, her agonized screams echoing through the chamber until they were silenced forever, leaving behind only a gaping void of horror and despair.

As the events unfolded, the men found themselves grappling with the aftermath of the goddess's ruthless attack on Paul's mother, Carter's wife. With a sense of urgency, Jack rushed to replace the displaced crystal, but the goddess, keenly aware of his actions, effortlessly pinned him against the wall with a forceful blow. In a desperate attempt to restrain her, William and Roger attempted to ensnare her with chains, only to watch in disbelief as the metal melted like wax in their hands.

Undeterred by the perilous situation, Carter and Dave launched themselves at the goddess, brandishing their weapons in a bold display of defiance. However, before they could strike, she vanished into thin air, leaving behind a sense of foreboding and chaos. Meanwhile, William and Roger were writhing in agony from their failed attempt to restrain her. Dave led them to the spigot on the front of the large glass vessel. "Hold your hands under here," Dave instructed, twisting it on full. An air of apprehension hung among them as they exchanged nervous glances. "Are you sure about this?" Roger's voice carried a hint of doubt.

"Yes, just for a short time. Hurry," Dave urged, his tone urgent, as they both plunged their hands into the cosmic stream and withdrew them just as quickly. A wave of relief washed over them as they watched their hands heal immediately.

"Who was that?" William's voice broke the silence, echoing in the chamber.

"I don't think any of us know who that was," Dave replied, his brow furrowed with uncertainty.

"Well, we have a full vat, and the traitor is dealt with," Jack declared with conviction.

"Hey, man, take it easy," Dave interjected, his voice calming.

"Yeah, you're right. Sorry, Carter," Jack apologized, his words laced with remorse.

"No problem. She obviously lost it somewhere," Carter remarked, his tone resigned.

"What was with Paul? Is he the half-blood child of Norakna? How did that work?" William's curiosity lingered in the air.

"Well, it would seem like he would be. As to how, I can't imagine, nor do I want to," Carter replied, his voice tinged with unease.

"Men, we have the ultimate elixir," Dave announced, drawing their attention to the swirling glass containing the blood of a very mighty god, the mightiest they had ever fought.

"We don't have to do this anymore after this," Dave continued.

"You know as well as I do, that we would have lost if it were not for Alzor," William reminded them.

"Do we owe him now?" Jack asked.

"No, we don't. My wife already paid for it," Carter clarified.

"So, we could drink the elixir just us and live freely?" Jack proposed.

"Yes, it would seem that way. But what about Paul? He looked pretty mad at the whole thing," Roger observed.

"Put the crystal back in, Jack," Carter instructed. Jack complied.

"Where does the safety go that your wife used?" Jack inquired.

"To the ethereal," Carter replied.

As they deliberated their next move, a sudden and violent onslaught against their protective wards jolted them into a state of heightened alertness. The relentless barrage intensified, each thunderous impact reverberating through the chamber like the primal fury of a wild beast yearning to get in. Before their eyes, the crystalline defenses shattered, rendered powerless against the unseen force that besieged them.

In the wake of this abrupt breach, the goddess reappeared, her ethereal presence casting a mesmerizing aura of both awe and trepidation. With disarming grace, and a kindly smile, she addressed them, "Can we agree to refrain from fighting or deceiving each other? I have a proposition for you, gentlemen," she said. The men remained in shock, astounded by her ability to dismantle their wards and safeties. Stepping forward, Dave spoke, "We will hear it." She turned her gaze towards Carter, stating, "I am speaking to the one whose son holds my companion's power within him." Carter, puzzled, inquired, "What do you mean? Is he not Norakna's child?" Her smile widened, "There are ways to separate the two from each other. Your wretched wife is human. I can sever the connection, and both of us can attain what we desire," she explained.

In the midst of uncertainty, the men found themselves at a crossroads, grappling with the weight of their decisions and the unforeseen consequences that lay ahead. The goddess's enigmatic offer loomed large, promising a path fraught with both peril and possibility.

Carter's gaze shifted from his companions to the enigmatic figure before him, his voice heavy with uncertainty. "Will he remain himself? Will he retain his memories?" he inquired, probing for assurances in the face of their unprecedented venture.

The goddess met his gaze with a serene assurance. "He will be as you desire," she assured him, her words carrying an otherworldly weight. Her next question hung in the air, a silent challenge to their resolve. "Will you grant him the elixir?" she asked, her tone a gentle reminder of the gravity of their choices.

Carter's response came without hesitation. "Of course," he affirmed, his commitment unwavering despite the weight of moral scrutiny.

However, the goddess's admonition resonated within the room, a stark reminder of their transgressions.

"You know, this is something that should not be," she began, her voice carrying the weight of ages. "You are cheating life cycles. It's against the laws for your kind; they have been put in place for reasons beyond your mortal scope."

At that point, the air in the room grew tense, thick with the gravity of her words.

Then, she smiled again, a sardonic twist to her lips. "Oh well, I guess as long as you leave us alone now since you will not have to do this anymore, am I correct?" she said, her tone dripping with irony.

Carter and his companions agreed to her terms. In a stunning display of her power, the goddess summoned forth a three-dimensional tableau of the ethereal realm, a living tapestry of cosmic energy that enveloped the room in its spectral embrace.

"Search for him," Carter implored his comrades, their collective gaze fixated on the swirling expanse of the ethereal plane. Meanwhile, the goddess stood at the epicenter, her breath weaving through the luminous fabric of the holographic display like a spectral beacon.

As the ethereal currents coalesced into a singular focal point, the goddess's revelation cast a pall of unease over their assembly. "He resides within the presence of an ancient, primordial being," she explained, her words laden with ominous portent. "You have called them black holes," she added, her tone tinged with a somber gravity.

Carter's incredulity was palpable as he grappled with the implications of her revelation. "My son... within a black hole?" he murmured. "Things are seen differently here, you know this." she retorted.

Yet, the goddess's reply offered little reassurance, leaving them to confront the harrowing reality of their predicament. "But he has the power of Norakna, does he not?" Jack inquired, his tone tinged with curiosity and concern.

"Some, yes, but he has no idea how to use it," she replied, her voice carrying a sense of urgency. "He is a child with godly power; his mind is still fragile. We must go now."

With a solemn nod, the goddess signaled their departure, summoning forth a tempest of swirling winds that enveloped their surroundings. In an instant, they were whisked away, transported to the very precipice of cosmic oblivion, where a titanic beast loomed large, its presence an awe-inspiring testament to the vastness and unfathomable mysteries of the cosmos.

The men stood in awe of the colossal being before them, its presence defying comprehension. She cloaked them from the beast, yet her signature could not be entirely masked. As they stood in her protective aura, the beast sensed her presence, and an incredibly low rumble vibrated through the ethereal realm. The intensity of the sound shook the men to their very bones.

"Melish, have you come for the boy who bears Norakna's power?" the creature intoned, its voice a deep, deliberate cadence that seemed to echo from the depths of eternity.

"Yes, I have," Melish replied, her tone unwavering in the face of the creature's imposing presence. "You know Taraq no longer holds sway over these realms."

The creature's response was swift, its voice rising to a crescendo of defiance. "No one rules me, Melish. You know this," it declared, its words a thunderous proclamation of autonomy.

Melish offered a knowing smile, her confidence unshaken by the creature's bluster. "Indeed, majestic one. Yet, you reside within his domain. Would it not follow that he holds dominion over you?" she countered, her voice calm amidst the tumultuous exchange.

Once more, the ethereal plane quaked with the force of the creature's fury as it grappled with her words. "And who now rules this domain?" it demanded, its voice dripping with disdain.

"It is Alzor, my lord," Melish replied, her words punctuated by the weight of truth.

The creature's reaction was immediate, a visceral expression of rage that threatened to tear the very fabric of reality asunder. "I despise that god! How can he claim dominion here?" it roared its voice a tempest of indignation.

But Melish remained steadfast, her resolve unyielding in the face of the creature's fury. "The circumstances of his rule are not our concern. Do you seek to change it, oh great void?" she inquired, her gaze unwavering as she met the creature's gaze.

His voice resonated low, slow, and mighty as he responded, "Yes, I do." Then, with unwavering determination, she asserted, "Then you must surrender the boy to me."

In a moment of reluctant acquiescence, the creature extended one of its massive tendrils, releasing Paul into the ethereal plane. "Take him," it rumbled.

As Paul floated before her, Melish posed a final question to the creature. "Would you lay claim to this domain?" she asked, her voice carrying the weight of destiny.

With a mighty roar that echoed across the vast expanse of the ethereal realm, the creature's response echoed through the void, its words a proclamation of intent that reverberated through the very fabric of existence.

A deep, rumbling laugh echoed from the colossal beast, filling the ethereal space with its ominous resonance. "No, my dear. I am but a wanderer of domains, a sentinel of the void," it declared, its voice carrying the weight of eons past. "Choose wisely, for my patience with gods like him wears thin. Should I consume him, it shall ignite a war for this realm, shattering my peace."

Melish regarded the creature with a sly grin, her eyes gleaming with mischief. "I have a proposition, my lord," she began, her tone laced with intrigue. "But I must confess, the man you have released to me is a

Molkien, as are these men," she continued, unveiling them before the creature.

The beast's disdain was palpable as it beheld the Molkiens. "Ah, Melish. I abhor them as much as I do Alzor—filthy thieves, disrupting the natural order," it growled, its voice dripping with contempt. "Is this truly your approach?"

Undeterred, Melish met the creature's gaze with unwavering resolve. "Do you trust me, ancient one?" she pressed, her words hanging in the air like a challenge.

For a moment, silence engulfed the ethereal plane. Then, without a word, the creature seemed to implode upon itself, vanishing into the void. There was a knowing between them.

Melish turned to the men, a smirk playing upon her lips. "That went better than expected," she remarked casually, before turning her attention to Paul, drawing him close.

Though unconscious, Paul emitted a faint bluish glow, a testament to the power coursing within him. "We must proceed to the extraction room," Melish announced, her voice commanding authority.

As they arrived at the chamber, she wasted no time in placing Paul within the immense glass container. "Stand back," she instructed, her tone brooking no argument. The men complied, watching with bated breath as Paul's body began to expand, the cosmic liquid within the glass diminishing rapidly.

Confusion gripped Dave as he found himself unable to move forward. "What's happening? You said no tricks!" he protested, his voice tinged with frustration.

Melish halted, her gaze piercing through the fabric of reality. "There will be ample for your needs. He must be immersed in the essence of the king before," she explained cryptically, before turning her focus back to Paul.

Suddenly, a blinding light erupted from the glass, dazzling the onlookers. In an instant, the brilliance vanished, and before them stood Norakna in all his majestic splendor.

He gazed at Melish, a mix of remorse and resignation evident in his eyes. "Oh, my love, what can I say? Weakness befell me," the mighty god confessed, his head bowed in shame. Melish stepped forward, gently lifting his chin with her hand. "No need for shame, my king. We have business to attend to," she reassured him, her voice firm and unwavering.

Stepping away from her, he addressed the men, who could now move freely. "Molkiens, today marks your end," the god declared, his voice echoing with authority.

"No, my love. They will trouble us no more," Melish interjected, her gaze piercing through the tension. "Do not force me to recount your misdeeds, my king. Leave them be, and let us focus on our tasks at hand."

The smoke from the god's nostrils subsided, and he offered a subtle wink to Carter, who contained his fury and remained silent. "Remember, Molkiens, stay away. I assure you, none will be playing nice," Melish warned, her tone leaving no room for argument.

With that, the two immortals vanished from sight. Amidst the commotion, Paul lay unconscious in front of the glass container. Carter rushed to his side, relieved to find him unharmed. Meanwhile, William retrieved a large glass vial and carefully transferred the remaining elixir from the container into it.

"She did leave us enough for ourselves," William remarked, breaking the somber silence that had settled over the group. "Let's depart. We should leave this place," Dave suggested, the weight of recent events heavy on his mind.

Opting for surface travel, they departed in their vehicles, the journey filled with a solemn quiet as each man wrestled with his thoughts. Upon reaching Carter's residence, they laid Paul down to rest while the others gathered around to discuss the implications of their newfound situation.

William placed the vial on the table, prompting a tense silence to descend upon the group. "Let's proceed," he urged, but no one spoke up. Sensing the hesitation, Dave turned to Carter, seeking clarity. "Are we going to administer the elixir to Paul?" he inquired.

Before Carter could respond, William interjected with a solemn revelation. "I've calculated, and I regret to inform you, Carter, that there are only enough doses left in the vial for five of us, at least if we wish to achieve the desired effect," he disclosed, his words hanging heavily in the air.

Carter let out a weary sigh, "I'll give it to him. I've lived long enough, I'm okay with it. Besides, I still have about 300 years left, right?" he joked.

"No, we don't. Your wife watered down our portions, I'm sure of it," Dave interjected, his tone serious. The others nodded in agreement, sensing that something was amiss this time. It was a brief burst of energy, unlike their previous experiences.

"But then who knows when you could die," Jack added.

Carter shrugged, offering a reassuring smile. "I feel fine, boys. Drink up. I'll give Paul his share."

William poured the elixir into silver goblets, and Carter fetched one for Paul, who was still asleep when his father entered the room. Carter nudged him gently. "Hey kiddo, wake up," he said softly.

Paul groggily opened his eyes, feeling a bit disoriented but surprisingly good. "Here, drink this. It'll make you feel better," his father said, handing him the goblet filled with the blood of a god. Paul, too thirsty to hesitate, eagerly gulped it down.

"How long have I been out? Is the party still going?" Paul asked, his memory fuzzy.

His father, taken aback by Paul's lack of recollection, hesitated before answering. "No, everyone has long gone home," he replied.

"I didn't embarrass myself, did I? Because I don't remember anything past the speeches," Paul continued, concern creeping into his voice.

His father chuckled softly. "Well then, you must have had a good time," he remarked with a hint of amusement.

"Yeah, I guess I did. You had some interesting guests," Paul remarked, his curiosity piqued.

"We did," his father agreed. "Get some more rest if you need it. I and the others are in the next room," he added before leaving Paul to rest.

"I'm good," Paul declared, rising to join the others. As he sat down, he began rummaging through his pockets in search of his phone. "Hey Dad, do you know where my phone might be?" he inquired.

"I think your mother sent the help to get you a new one, son. You had dropped yours," his father explained. He then excused himself to speak with the help. When he returned, he had a brand-new phone in hand. "Here you go, Paul. Brand new," he announced.

Paul eagerly accepted the phone and started checking his messages. "I have to go. Thanks for the great night, Dad. Thank Mom too. And see you guys. It was a pleasure to have met you. You are probably the most interesting people I have ever met," Paul said as he shook their hands, hugged his father, and left.

Upon arriving at Jeremy's place, Paul went straight inside. Jeremy was surrounded by piles of documents and pictures scattered across the table. "What are you talking about?" Paul inquired.

"Paul, sit down. You have to see this. Your family is old, and I mean ancient, Paul. Look," Jeremy urged, gesturing towards pictures of ruins he had been excavating. "They're bad, Paul. They drain the blood of gods to live longer. I've been trying to get a hold of you for a few days," Jeremy explained urgently.

"A few days? That doesn't make sense. I was at a family party last night. I talked to you before I left," Paul protested, confused.

"No, Paul. That was a few days ago," Jeremy insisted.

Paul sat down, taking in everything Jeremy had collected and listening to his theory. When Jeremy finished, Paul leaned back, placing his head in his hands, lost in thought. "Or at least that's how I am seeing it," Jeremy added.

"Now what?" Paul asked, feeling overwhelmed.

"I don't know," Jeremy admitted. "Do you think they are still doing it?" he inquired.

"How would I know?" Paul replied, his mind racing with possibilities. Panicking inside, he blurted out, "What if we poison them?"

Jeremy looked at him aghast. "Are you crazy? No, no," Jeremy exclaimed.

"If what you are saying is true, they should be alright," Paul said calmly.

"Yeah, but what if I am wrong, Paul?" Jeremy questioned, his voice tinged with worry.

"I believe you are right," Paul said in desperation. "Does it say anything in the texts on how to test for it?" he asked.

"No, but you can't, Paul," Jeremy protested.

Paul stared at Jeremy intently. "Okay, we could use a recipe I did find among the same fragments. However, Paul, if they are not what you think, they will drop dead instantly, and you will be a murderer," Jeremy warned.

Paul heard nothing except that there was a recipe. "Mix it up," he insisted.

"Okay, but this will be on you if it goes bad," Jeremy said, his disbelief evident. Yet, he was curious, and there was a lingering sense of certainty in Paul's conviction. He went to his pantry, filled with many exotic and strange things, pulled out some ingredients, and started mixing and mashing until he had a clear, odorless liquid. Jeremy poured it into a long, thin vial and capped it. "Here, it's yours now," he said, handing it to Paul.

Paul grabbed it eagerly, a smile creeping across his face. "Where's your good wine?" he asked.

Jeremy fetched his best wine. "Okay, let's go," Paul declared.

"No, I'm not coming," Jeremy protested.

"Yes, you are. Let's go," Paul insisted, and Jeremy, though hesitant, shrugged and followed Paul as they left for Paul's parents' house.

Once they arrived, Paul and Jeremy slipped in through the kitchen doors and poured the wine into glasses before bringing them into the sitting room. All the men were gathered there, and the timing could not have been more perfect—all their drinks were empty.

"Here, gentlemen, have a drink with me in celebration of a wonderful night and new friendships made," Paul announced as he and Jeremy handed out the drinks, ensuring theirs had none of the concoction.

Paul raised his glass, about to toast, when he realized his mother wasn't present. "Dad, where's Mom?" Paul asked his father.

"Ah, she is out, son," his father replied.

Paul raised his glass once again. "To good times and good friends. May we live forever," he said, and they all drank up.

As they drank, Paul scrutinized them intently, searching for any sign of effect. None of them seemed affected. "Aha, I knew it," he started to say, but then his father's head fell onto the table. Paul's gaze shot to his father, and in an instant, he witnessed a bizarre transformation. His father's skin shimmered, taking on a strange texture resembling stone scales, and then just as quickly, it flashed back to normal. Paul blinked and rubbed his eyes in disbelief. The others had already gathered around Paul's father, while Paul could only look on in horror at what he had done. He was sure, but he was wrong, but the rest of them were fine.

"He's gone," Dave said, breaking the stunned silence. William ran over to Paul, his voice rising with anger. "What was in those drinks, boy?" he demanded.

"I just wanted to see if you were immortal. I thought we were right," Paul explained, his voice trembling with guilt.

"Yes, Paul, we are. You are. But your father was on borrowed time at this point, or that's what we had been thinking. There was only enough elixir for us, but he gave his portion to you," Dave explained, his tone heavy with regret.

Paul couldn't believe what had just happened; his head was reeling. William stepped aside as Dave guided Paul to a seat, urging him to relax. "We have some things to tell you," Dave said, his gaze serious as the rest of the group looked on. "William and Roger, you need to attend to Carter according to the plan," Dave instructed solemnly.

Dave and Jack explained the situation to Paul and Jeremy, outlining the truth about his mother and why his father couldn't handle the drink, Paul listened in silence, processing everything. "So, William and Roger put my dad in a preservation casket?" Paul asked, seeking confirmation.

"Yes, we believe it can preserve him until we submerge him in the elixir," Dave confirmed.

"But there's no more elixir, right?" Paul inquired.

"No, but we could get more if we dared to do so," Jack suggested.

"Or you could just let him rest. He has lived a very long and good life," Jeremy interjected, offering a different perspective.

William and Roger returned, nodding at Dave, who returned the gesture. "Paul's friend Jeremy says we should let Carter rest in peace," Dave announced, mockingly.

William and Roger's laughter echoed through the room. "You see, boy, we don't do that," Roger stated with a smirk, his tone dripping with mockery. Jeremy glanced back at the others, finding their expressions filled with disappointment, their heads shaking in disapproval. "Paul, say something," Jeremy pleaded, desperation lacing his voice.

Paul, sensing the weight of the moment, rose from his seat. As if the gravity of the situation had ignited the immortal spark within him, fire blazed in his eyes, a fierce determination emanating from his gaze. Without hesitation, he reached for his dimensional weapon, raising it high above his head.

"We don't do that."

The Forgotten Pack

He pressed himself against the rough brick wall outside the entrance of the club, opposite the imposing doorman bouncer. Wolf, just as colossal as the bouncer, stood at an impressive 6 foot 4 inches tall and weighed a solid 280 pounds, with muscles chiseled from stone and a merciless demeanor. However, they were both on the same team. Wolf worked as the inside bouncer, specifically for the private rooms, ensuring that things never got out of hand. He took out a cigarette, lit it up, and engaged in some idle chatter with the other bouncer before leaning against the wall, silently observing as the patrons streamed into the club. Wolf despised the crowd that frequented the establishment, but it afforded him a place to live, some cash, and kept him in excellent physical condition.

As the people continued to enter, Wolf's mind raced. He had a knack for sensing troublemakers and could discern who would cause problems in the club. He crushed his cigarette underfoot, acknowledged the doorman with a nod, and followed a group of three individuals who had just entered. He reported to the floor bouncer, alerting him about whom to keep an eye on, before striding towards a large, red door at the back of the club. The door swung open, revealing a gargantuan man. Wolf acknowledged him with a nod before proceeding down a poorly lit corridor.

Suddenly, a buzzer went off, and a green light flickered on. Someone had rented one of the exclusive private rooms for the night. The clients who reserved these rooms were often obscenely wealthy, leading to some crazy situations. Wolf often had to let things slide, but when the safety of the girls was at stake, he wouldn't hesitate to intervene. Depending on the issue, things could escalate rapidly, and Wolf's reputation as "Wolf" was not unfounded.

He slipped into the room through a separate entrance, far removed from the girls and the clients. Initially, the girls were kept behind glass until the clients summoned them into the room. Upon entry, he surveyed the room, noting that no one was present. He positioned himself menacingly in the corner, his long black hair concealing his face like a hood. He wore a black canvas trench coat that trailed the floor, its leather lining gleaming under the dim lighting.

Soon, the clients arrived, as drunk as ever. Seven of them, two of whom did not appear to be present for pleasure. Their shock at seeing Wolf standing there was palpable. "Who are you?" one of them inquired, to which Wolf responded calmly, "Security."

"We have our own security," the man replied, gesturing to Hal and Jim. "They'll take care of everything. You can go."

A smirk played on Wolf's lips. "Well, if I leave, the girls don't come out. We have an arrangement."

One of the other men whispered something in the first man's ear. "Yeah, whatever. Stay. We don't care," he said dismissively.

Wolf nodded, his hand moving to a red button on the wall beside him. As he pressed it, the curtain separating the girls from the clients parted, revealing the women. The night progressed as expected, with the wealthy and corrupt reveling in their depravity. Wolf marveled at the depths some people could sink, but he paid them little heed, so long as they did not harm the ladies.

Eventually, one of the men grew increasingly rough with one of the girls and pulled out a weapon. Wolf sprang into action, disarming the brute with ease.

Wolf's attention was drawn to the sudden commotion in the room, as both bodyguards made their move towards him. The one in front was sprinting faster and seemed like he would reach Wolf first. Wolf delivered a hard kick just above the pubic bone of the oncoming bodyguard, causing him to double over in agony. Before the guy could regain his balance, Wolf struck him with a powerful knee to the head, knocking him out cold.

As the second bodyguard rushed in from the back, Wolf pivoted on his left foot, bringing his right leg back and to the side, and delivering a devastating kick to the knee of the oncoming bodyguard. The force of the blow was enough to bring the guy down, and Wolf followed through with an elbow to the jaw, knocking him out cold as well. All the while, he had not let go of the man whose arm he was holding.

The rest of the partygoers were shouting at Wolf to let their friend go, but he silenced them with a finger to his lips. "Treat the girls with respect," Wolf growled. The guy whose arm he was holding stammered nervously, "Yeah, for sure, sorry I got out of hand."

"Don't tell me, tell her," Wolf said, gesturing towards the woman. The guy apologized to the woman, and Wolf released him. The party resumed, and the two knocked-out bodyguards had gotten up and were nursing their wounds, trying their best to avoid looking at Wolf.

Wolf returned to his corner, confident that there would be no more trouble from these clients. As a matter of fact, they made it an early night and paid extra for the room of their own accord. The owner of the club walked up to Wolf, a mix of curiosity and concern etched on his face.

"What did you do to those boys, Wolf? They were scared shitless," he asked.

"You know the usual," Wolf replied with a shrug.

"Right, whatever. Here's your cut, good job. The ladies thank you, as usual," the owner said, handing Wolf his payment. Wolf grinned, his long black hair falling over his face like a hood, as he pocketed the cash.

In the dimly lit room, Wolf stepped out, leaving behind the last room of the night. His intention was clear: to quench his thirst at his favored watering hole, a place more rugged than the club he worked at, and home to bands with a harder edge that resonated with his personal taste. Exiting through the front doors, he encountered a group of troublemakers engaged in a heated exchange with both the bouncers inside and outside the establishment. Undeterred, Wolf maneuvered his way between them, swiftly delivering a devastating blow to the man on his right, followed by a forceful stomp on the knee of his left adversary, causing him to collapse in agony. Before the remaining troublemaker could react, the vigilant inside bouncer apprehended him, cautioning against any ill-advised confrontation.

"You'd be wise not to tangle with him," the bouncer warned.

"I wasn't planning to. I was going to make a run for it," admitted the frightened young man.

"Good. Don't dally here any longer, now go," the bouncer advised, as Wolf had already departed, lost in his thoughts about the bands performing that night.

His regular workplace closed its doors at 3 a.m., but the place he was headed to remained open until sunrise or 7 a.m., whichever came last. The street was littered with inebriated individuals making their way from the club, yet their presence did not faze Wolf. Most of them had grown accustomed to his familiar figure. The journey to his destination took a mere half an hour, and upon arrival, he was warmly greeted by the door bouncer.

"Evening, Wolf. Good to see you," acknowledged the door bouncer.

Wolf nodded in acknowledgment and made his way inside. He occupied a seat that remained unoccupied until his customary arrival. As he proceeded to his designated spot, he received numerous nods of recognition and friendly greetings. The venue buzzed with activity during the intermission between bands, a bustling atmosphere that Wolf was well acquainted with.

The drinks were delivered to him by the waitress, her demeanor laced with flirtatiousness. "Hi, Wolf. How are you doing tonight?" she inquired, a playful twinkle in her eyes.

"Good, and how about you, Candy?" he responded.

"Oh, you know, pretty good. It's a little wild here tonight. Had to fend off a few handsy guys. Big Jim and Riley have tossed out at least six people so far," she divulged. Wolf chuckled, appreciating the chaotic nature of the evening.

"Sounds like it's been a good night then," he remarked.

"Yep, now that you're here, it is," she said, her lips curling into a smile. "Later, Wolf. I'll only be serving you for another hour, and then the new girl will take over," she informed him.

He grinned mischievously. "This should be fun," he uttered.

"Be nice," she playfully scolded, wagging her finger at him before departing. Wolf reclined in his seat, sipping his shots and settling into his drink. The next band took the stage, drawing a gathering crowd. Wolf eagerly anticipated the impending onslaught, and he was not disappointed. As the first chord reverberated through the air, he became consumed by the raw intensity. The band unleashed a brutal and unyielding sound that engulfed him entirely. He sat there, a smile adorning his face, eyes closed, lost in the music. Though his physical presence remained in the room, his mind detached itself, allowing him to transcend the realm.

Lost in this ethereal space, Wolf could lose track of time as long as the band played. His consciousness drifted, and at some point, a small voice broke through the cacophony. "Can I get you anything, Mr. Wolf?" The unexpected intrusion jolted him back to reality, and he opened his eyes to behold the loveliest woman he had ever laid eyes upon.

"Um, yes, I'll have three more tequila shots and two double whiskeys," he ordered. Curiosity piqued, he inquired, "What's your name?"

A shy smile adorned her face as she replied, "My name is Rachel."

"Hi, Rachel. I'm Wolf," he introduced himself.

"Wolf? That's a cool name," she remarked. "I'll go get your drinks, Wolf," she said before swiftly departing. Wolf couldn't help but notice the uniqueness of Rachel. She seemed different from the other girls who worked here, even different from the ones at his club. There was an air of innocence about her that intrigued him.

Moments later, Rachel returned, drinks in hand. "Thank you," Wolf expressed his gratitude.

She giggled softly. "It's my job," she replied, her eyes sparkling with mirth. "You're welcome, of course," Rachel replied before turning and departing. Wolf yearned to engage in further conversation, but he recognized the validity of her words—she was there to work. Downing his shots in swift succession, he remained immersed in the relentless energy of the band's performance. The mosh pit had reached an uncontrollable fervor. While he longed to join the chaotic fray, he refrained, fearing unintentional harm. However, the true motive behind his restraint was to keep his gaze fixed upon Rachel. She lingered persistently in his thoughts, an enigmatic presence.

Wolf observed her discreetly, attempting to remain inconspicuous. Yet, the astute bartender discerned his intentions and approached him. "She's single, in case you were wondering. Dude, you're not being too subtle," he jested, laughter lacing his words.

Wolf erupted into laughter. "Man, I can't help it," he admitted. The bartender joined in his amusement. "She was already inquiring about you, so no worries. Just don't come off too stalkerish," he advised.

Wolf smiled and nodded, but his eyes never wavered from Rachel's figure. Then, a troubling incident unfolded—a group of individuals at a nearby table began harassing her. The club's security personnel swiftly intervened. Wolf fixated on the scene like a famished predator, his anticipation palpable. He leaned forward in his chair, teetering on the edge of involvement, yet striving to exercise restraint.

It seemed as though the matter had been resolved, with Rachel having already distanced herself from the table. The security team turned to walk away, believing the situation to be diffused. However, two individuals positioned at the far end of the table seized empty bottles and launched an ambush on the unsuspecting bouncers. But before their attack could land, Wolf was already upon them, seizing their arms and delivering swift, decisive blows. He locked eyes with the remaining individuals seated at the table, his gaze a potent mixture of menace and ferocity.

"Do you know who I am? Do you?" one of the men at the table bellowed at Wolf. Before another word escaped his lips, Wolf leaped over the table, pouncing upon the man's chair, relentlessly pummeling him into submission. The two companions adjacent to him attempted to strike Wolf but found themselves ensnared in the crossfire of their friend's punishment, subjected to a barrage of punishing blows. Having incapacitated their friend, Wolf proceeded to dispatch the remaining assailants with unwavering brutality. When he finally rose from behind the table, his body was drenched in a macabre tapestry of crimson. The security personnel swiftly intervened, dragging the fallen troublemakers outside into the parking lot. As Wolf walked away, they apprehended the remaining individuals, meting out the same fate. A sense of triumph surged through him, his adrenaline-fueled euphoria soaring to new heights. Seeking to cleanse himself of the bloodshed, he made his way to the restroom, causing all occupants to hurriedly vacate.

As he washed away the remnants of the skirmish, the sound of the door swinging open seized his attention. He spun around, his eyes locking onto Rachel's figure standing before him. Concern etched across her face, she cautiously approached. "Are you okay?" she inquired, her voice laced with genuine worry.

Wolf offered a reassuring smile. "I'm fine. Sorry, you had to witness that," he responded, gratitude evident in his tone.

"Thank you so much. When I'm working, your drinks are on the house," she offered, a gesture of appreciation.

"No, no, it's not necessary," Wolf insisted. After a brief, awkward pause, they both emerged from the restroom. Wolf returned to his seat, and Rachel followed suit. He still had a drink and a half left, which he swiftly consumed. Rachel swiftly attended to his usual order upon his nonverbal request. When she returned, he reached for his wallet to settle the bill, but she vehemently refused. The band had continued to play throughout the entire ordeal, lending an air of epicness to the scene. Wolf remained seated until the first rays of dawn pierced the sky, signaling the end of the final band's performance. Satisfied, he resolved it was time to head home.

Inebriated from the copious amount of drinks Rachel had provided, Wolf made his way towards the exit. However, Rachel intercepted him before he could depart. "Hey, need some company?" she offered, her voice filled with a subtle longing.

"No, I'm good. I'll see you tomorrow," he declined, his speech slightly slurred as he stepped through the doorway. In his current state, he lacked the clarity to properly escort her home, but he couldn't deny a growing desire for their paths to cross again. Stumbling through the streets, Wolf eventually reached his abode—an apartment located above the club where he toiled. Exhaustion gripped him swiftly, lulling him into a deep slumber.

The band's preparations for the evening show roused him from his sleep. Rising from his bed, he indulged in a meal, engaged in some physical training, and then cleansed himself under the shower's refreshing spray. Wolf readied himself for another night of work, feeling surprisingly well despite the copious libations of the previous night. Descending the stairs within the club, he was greeted warmly by his fellow employees, a sense of camaraderie permeating the atmosphere. Wolf made his way to his customary refuge behind the scenes, tucked away in the labyrinthine back rooms. Only three other individuals shared this domain with him, and while they couldn't match Wolf's unruly toughness, they formed a formidable group of rowdy characters. He appreciated their presence and, as he entered, they greeted him with genuine camaraderie. Engrossed in lively banter, they regaled each other with tales of the previous night's escapades. However, their conversation abruptly ceased as the buzzers echoed throughout the room, signaling the end of their camaraderie. They bid their farewells and dispersed to their respective chambers.

The night progressed in a whirlwind, with the clientele exhibiting a semblance of normalcy that surprised Wolf. The final stretch was within reach, and he found himself on his last break before attending to one last room. If the night continued to unfold as smoothly as it had thus far, he would consider it a resounding success. Yet, deep down, he knew all too well that life rarely unfolded so neatly.

One of the floor bouncers made his way to Wolf, approaching with a purpose. "Hey, there's been a girl waiting to see you most of the night. I know you've been busy, but I told her I'd check if she could see you," the bouncer informed him. A smile crept across Wolf's face. "Yeah, man, let her in," he replied. The bouncer nodded and departed, swiftly returning with Rachel by his side. Her beaming countenance radiated joy as she greeted him. "I've been waiting to see you. How are you?" she inquired, her voice brimming with genuine interest.

"Doing good, it's been a pleasant night so far," Wolf responded, his tone reflecting his satisfaction. Curiosity piqued, he asked, "What brings you here?"

Rachel blushed slightly, her cheeks tinged with a hint of bashfulness. "I wanted to come to see you. I had some free time before work," she confessed. They engaged in a leisurely conversation, savoring each moment shared. However, their respite was interrupted by the sound of the buzzer, accompanied by a vivid green light illuminating one of the doors. "Okay, I have to go. See you at The Pit," Wolf declared. Rachel's smile persisted. "Yeah, you will," she responded, bidding him farewell before departing.

Wolf felt a subtle disarray within, captivated by the enigmatic allure of this intriguing woman. He shrugged off his unease, adopting his customary game face as he prepared to tackle the impending task at hand. With unwavering resolve, he stepped through the door adorned with the beckoning green light. Once inside, he executed his customary routine, poised and patient, awaiting the arrival of the clients. The door swung open, revealing five men entering the room. Among them, two appeared inebriated and of diminutive stature, while the remaining trio stood towering and resolute, stone-cold sober. As the men's gazes fell upon Wolf, they engaged in hushed conversations, punctuated by boisterous laughter. Unperturbed, Wolf paid them no mind. "Come on, man! Bring on the girls!" one of the smaller men bellowed with impatience. Wolf simply nodded, reaching out to press the button that lifted the veil, revealing three enticing dancers gracefully moving to the rhythm.

For a while, the proceedings followed their familiar course. However, an unexpected shift occurred when the conversation among the girls took an eerie turn. The smaller man seized one of the dancers, gently placing her on his lap. "Hey, can I tell you a story?" he asked, a mischievous glint in his eyes. She giggled, her curiosity piqued. "Sure."

And so, he commenced his tale—a tale of a monstrous man and the heinous deeds wrought by his monstrous hands. The other small man burst into laughter. "Have you ever heard anything so preposterous?" he scoffed, his voice laced with incredulity. Echoing his companion's sentiments, he chimed in, "What a joke! People and their stories."

The girl joined in the laughter, seemingly amused by the narrative. "People do tell stories, huh, Wolf?" one of them jeered, provoking a reaction. Wolf remained silent, a cryptic smile lingering on his lips. Sensing their opportunity, the men persisted, mocking him with their raucous laughter. "Oh, another story about our dear Wolf," one taunted, their mockery echoing through the room.

Their relentless jibes continued, exacerbating the tense atmosphere. Then, the man with the girl on his lap abruptly brandished a gun, pressing it against her delicate temple. The room fell into stunned silence as his voice resonated with a cold, measured tone. "What are you gonna do now, tough guy? Those guys you roughed up last night, one of them was my brother. You've stirred the hornet's nest, Wolf and my family aren't one to be trifled with."

Wolf, no longer a mere fixture against the wall, emerged as a commanding presence, his aura radiating authority. "I will count to three," he declared, his voice laced with an unyielding edge. "Then what?" one of the men retorted, defiant and unyielding.

"You will find out soon enough if you don't drop that gun," Wolf warned his words carrying a menacing weight. He didn't bother to proceed to three; deep down, he knew this young man would not relinquish his grip without a fight. With astonishing speed and agility, Wolf lunged forward, sliding effortlessly between the towering figures before him. In a fluid motion, he unleashed a swift kick that propelled the chair backward, causing it to topple over. Seizing the opportune moment, he deftly entangled the armed man's arm, executing a series of precise maneuvers that rendered the young man helpless. With his knee pressed firmly against the intruder's back and a firm grip on his hair, Wolf forcefully slammed the cold metal barrel of the gun against the back of his skull.

Perhaps, under different circumstances, he might have relented, allowing the young man a reprieve. But time was of the essence; the others were closing in, leaving Wolf with no choice but to act swiftly. One resounding gunshot echoed through the room, silencing the young man's threats forever. The three larger adversaries met a similar fate, their lives abruptly cut short by the lethal precision of Wolf's shots. However, he intentionally spared the remaining small man, leaving him to witness the aftermath of his failed endeavor.

Enveloped in a fiery rage, Wolf approached the trembling survivor, his gaze piercing into the depths of the man's soul. "Tell me the reason behind this madness," Wolf demanded, his voice carrying an air of controlled menace. Shaking uncontrollably, the man managed to stammer a response, revealing the purpose of their ill-fated mission. "We were sent here to give you a severe beating," he confessed, his fear palpable. "You've harmed someone of great importance. Our organization deemed it fitting to deliver a warning, a beating, or a gunshot, but not death," he explained, desperate to save his own life.

A wicked smile curled upon Wolf's lips as he processed the information. "Empty your pockets, hand over all the money you possess, and make yourself scarce," he commanded with cold authority. The man complied, tremblingly thrusting a substantial bundle of cash into Wolf's awaiting grasp. "Here," he stammered, before hastily fleeing the room, desperate to escape the clutches of impending doom. Wolf carefully stowed the money in his pocket, his mind already shifting gears to the task at hand. It had been a while since he found himself in this situation, but he knew the drill all too well. Now, he had to tidy up the mess he had made. Leaving the room behind, he traversed the dimly lit back hallways, his steps purposeful and calculated. Seeking out the club owner, he relayed the events that had transpired, explaining how he had swiftly taken control of the situation, as he always did. The owner shook his head in a mixture of exasperation and admiration.

"What am I going to do with you, Wolf?" the owner sighed, a wry smile tugging at the corners of his lips. "Well, I'm just glad you're on my side. As unpredictable as you are, you get the job done," he chuckled before sauntering away, leaving Wolf to his grim duties.

Returning to the room, Wolf methodically placed each lifeless body into sturdy body bags, a somber reminder of the risks that accompanied his line of work. His boss had been wise enough to keep an ample supply on hand, recognizing their practicality in this macabre profession. With the bodies secured, Wolf shouldered the weight of his burdens and approached the bay doors. The waiting truck, its door ajar, beckoned him like an accomplice in his clandestine endeavors. He deposited the bags inside, closing the truck door with a resolute thud, sealing away the evidence of the night's violence. Wolf traversed the vast expanse of the arid desert, a desolate wasteland stretching out before him as far as the eye could see. Arriving at a secluded spot, carefully chosen, Wolf came to a halt.

Taking a moment to collect himself, Wolf stepped out of the vehicle and leaned casually against its front grill. Retrieving a cigarette from his pocket, he ignited it with a flick of his lighter, the glowing ember casting eerie shadows across his face. Inhaling deeply, he allowed the nicotine to soothe his frayed nerves before releasing a primal, blood-curdling howl into the night air. The sound reverberated through the desolate landscape, carrying both a sense of defiance and communion.

A pack of formidable wolves emerged from the shadows, their eyes gleaming with feral hunger. Their snarls and growls echoed through the stillness, a testament to their untamed nature. Wolf's smile widened, a flicker of excitement dancing in his eyes. Discarding his cigarette into the sandy ground, he addressed the pack with a mixture of reverence and authority.

"You came, as I knew you would. Good. I have something for you," he declared, his voice carrying a unique blend of respect and familiarity. Moving towards the back of the truck, he swung open the doors, revealing the lifeless forms within. With a swift motion, he released the bodies from their enclosures, presenting them as an offering to the voracious creatures.

"Feast!" Wolf commanded, his voice laced with a primal edge. The wolves responded with a resounding chorus of howls, their hunger overcoming any remnants of caution. They descended upon the bodies with an insatiable appetite, tearing into the flesh with untamed savagery. As Wolf observed the spectacle, a vehicle materialized on the outskirts, headlights cutting through the darkness. Stepping out from the vehicle, Rachel emerged, her presence a blend of curiosity and intrigue. As Rachel stepped forward, a primal fury ignited within the wolves. Their gnarled jaws contorted into ferocious snarls, their eyes ablaze with unyielding aggression. Wolf's voice pierced the tension-laden air, commanding them to halt their onslaught. A tense stillness settled upon the scene, with Rachel and the formidable beasts locked in a perilous standoff. Slowly, deliberately, Wolf made his way towards her, his gaze a mixture of bewilderment and concern.

"What are you doing here? How did you find me?" Wolf's words resonated with a blend of astonishment and apprehension, his voice laced with a tinge of disbelief. Rachel's response hung in the air, carrying the weight of her unwavering determination.

"I followed you, Wolf. I saw you climb into the truck and drive away, and I couldn't resist the urge to see where you were headed," she confessed, her voice unwavering yet tinged with a touch of vulnerability. The realization of her presence, so unexpected and yet undeniably present, left Wolf grappling with conflicting emotions.

"You shouldn't have come," he muttered, his voice a low rumble of uncertainty. His mind raced, contemplating the dangers that lurked within his world and the implications of Rachel entangling herself in his shadowed existence.

"I apologize," she whispered. Wolf embraced her tightly, and the wolves resumed their feasting. "It's too late for apologies now. You're here, and there's no need to worry," he assured her. She nestled closer to him as two SUVs pulled up. Wolf's expression turned unimpressed. He turned to Rachel and instructed, "Stay here. I'll be right back."

As he approached the vehicles, six men armed with automatic weapons emerged. An imposing older man, though physically strong, stepped out last, leaning on a walking stick he clearly didn't require. "Mr. Wolf, my boss would like to meet with you," he announced. The wolves had encircled them, but the armed men noticed and fired their weapons into the air, causing the wolves to scatter. Rachel walked up to Wolf and placed her hand on his shoulder. "Let's just go with them, Wolf," she urged.

Wolf was about to respond when he was struck with the butt end of a rifle. It didn't knock him out; instead, it ignited a furious rage within him. He retaliated by pummeling the assailant and engaging in a fierce battle with all of them. However, one of the men seized Rachel. "If you don't want me to shoot her, get in the damn vehicle now!" he threatened.

Wolf reluctantly halted his assault and climbed into one of the vehicles. The older man, accompanied by two others, joined him, while Rachel and the remaining captors occupied the second vehicle. Wolf remained silent, his gaze fixed on the old man. The old man showed no signs of being unsettled either. Not a word was spoken.

It had to be about what transpired the previous night and tonight. Wolf was prepared for whatever awaited him.

They arrived at a colossal hotel. "Alright, let's proceed," the older man declared. They exited the vehicles and made their way inside, stepping into an elevator. Still unable to catch a glimpse of Rachel, Wolf held onto the certainty that he would soon see her. Finally, they reached the top floor and were ushered into a spacious room adorned with three semi-circular couches and a grand desk crafted from leather and oak. Behind it sat a massive man with a tight white beard, short white hair, and eyes of parchment-like intensity. Flanking him on either side stood two men, while a shrouded figure occupied the space behind him to the right. Two chairs were brought forward and placed in front of the imposing desk.

"Sit," commanded the large man from his seat. Wolf took his place, and Rachel followed suit. The man's gaze fixated upon Wolf, scrutinizing him intensely. Yet, Wolf remained resolute, refusing to waver under the weight of that piercing stare.

"I can tell just by looking at you that you are a valiant and strong individual," the man spoke, his voice carrying a commanding authority. "Had my son not crossed the line, you wouldn't have needed to set him straight. My sons informed me of their plans for this evening, and I advised them against it. But, as you know, boys will be boys. Nevertheless, my friend, regardless of the danger posed, you killed my boy and returned to me a lifeless vessel."

He paused momentarily, his gaze never leaving Wolf's face. "Those boys are foolish, but they are still my sons," he continued. "Now, Mr. Wolf, what would you do in my position?"

Wolf shrugged nonchalantly, a hint of indifference in his response. "I have no children," he replied, his voice carrying a touch of detachment.

A faint smile curled upon the old man's lips. "Ah, but you are mistaken, Father," he uttered, his words laced with cryptic meaning. Wolf's gaze shifted between the old man and Rachel, his expression etched with confusion. "And your queen beside you," the old man stated, drawing attention to Rachel. She rose from her seat, her voice firm as she addressed Wolf. "Wolf, the time has come for you to answer for your crimes against our own kind. You fed us, men laden with poison, and we suffered immensely. We begged the lake gods for mercy, but they refused to aid us as they aided you. Desperate, we sought solace in the swamps, where we encountered the hag. She offered us a pact—one must be bound to the swamp. And we chose you, the one responsible for the devastation we endured. You will face the judgment of the lake gods and be cast into the swamp of the Hag," Rachel declared.

Wolf's mind reeled with disbelief. Who were these individuals, and what were they talking about? Madness seemed to permeate their words. He struggled to comprehend the situation unfolding before him. The shrouded figure, ancient in appearance yet possessing lively eyes, stepped forward. "He doesn't remember," the figure remarked, his voice carrying the weight of ages. "The lake gods willed it so. But surely, they did not anticipate that you would feed your own kind poison."

Wolf rose abruptly from his chair, his voice laced with frustration. "Enough with these riddles! Who are you people truly? What is this madness?" he demanded, his confusion giving way to a wave of simmering anger. The formidable older man rose from his seat, his movements fluid and powerful. With astonishing agility, he leaped onto the desk, and to Wolf's disbelief, he transformed into a massive black wolf adorned with striking white markings. Shocked and alarmed, Wolf instinctively recoiled, his voice echoing with incredulity. "What manner of sorcery is this?" he bellowed, his mind grappling to comprehend the extraordinary spectacle unfolding before him.

The older man, now in lupine form, retained his composed demeanor and spoke with an air of wisdom. "No sorcery, my dear Wolf. You were once a leader among wolves—a Wolf leader. But the lake gods decreed a different fate for you, transforming you into the man you are now," the ancient figure explained. With a swift shift, the wolf reverted back to its human form, settling comfortably into a seated position behind the desk. The room fell into a heavy silence, the weight of revelation settling upon Wolf's shoulders.

"I am no wolf, nor a werewolf. I am simply a regular human," Wolf protested, his voice tinged with uncertainty and defiance. The man behind the desk regarded him intently, his gaze penetrating. "Indeed, you are not a werewolf, nor do you possess the ability to shift into a wolf-like I just did. Yet, it remains an intrinsic part of who you are," he replied with a measured tone.

Wolf turned his attention to Rachel, who had resumed her seat. His eyes bore into hers, searching for answers. "So, this was all a ploy, a scheme to deceive and trap me?" he accused, his voice laced with a mix of anger and betrayal. Rachel's countenance softened, her lips curling into a captivating smile. "You were our king, our leader. But then you became the one who poisoned our pack—the pack that only Silas, Adolam, two others, and I remain a part of. Silas has assumed the mantle of pack leader. Those you beat and killed were our children," Rachel revealed, her words laden with a complex blend of sorrow and vengeance.

Her voice took on a wistful note as she continued, "We have created a new life for ourselves here, a life of prosperity. Why would we return to the harsh struggle of the desert, subsisting on rodents? We have found solace in our newfound existence."

The room grew heavy with the weight of secrets unveiled and destinies entwined.

The notion of exacting revenge surged through Wolf's mind, tempting him to eradicate every last one of them. Yet, their accusations struck a deep chord within him. The realization that his actions had inadvertently poisoned the very wolves he believed he was nourishing seeped into his consciousness, filling him with an overwhelming sense of guilt. He had never once considered the possibility, never fathomed the consequences of his deeds. The weight of this revelation bore down on him, and the rage that had welled up within him ebbed away, replaced by a mix of confusion and remorse.

The concept of him being a wolf, however, remained enigmatic and perplexing. True, the moniker "Wolf" had been bestowed upon him due to his macabre practice of feeding others to the wolves. Yet, only a select few were privy to the truth behind the name, while the majority simply referred to him as Wolf because it had stuck. He was not an actual wolf, he was a man—an ordinary man, or so he believed.

As if to further bewilder him, the ancient figure known as Adolam strode purposefully toward a distant wall. With swift motions, he cleared away various objects obstructing his path. From his pocket, he retrieved a small obsidian rock, roughly the size of an egg. Using the rock, he etched a grand arched doorway onto the surface. Intriguingly, Adolam then delved into his other pocket, producing a handful of vivid crimson powder, which he gracefully blew into the interior space of the arch. Wolf's eyes were fixated on the mesmerizing scene unfolding before him.

As the scarlet powder settled upon the wall, an ethereal transformation began to take shape. The surface shimmered and rippled, like a pond disturbed by a gentle breeze. Gradually, the wall within the arch morphed into a deep, inky blackness, an abyss that seemed to beckon Wolf into the unknown. The spectacle unfolded with an otherworldly aura, leaving Wolf both captivated and unnerved. What manner of arcane forces were these people entwined with? This question resonated within his mind, fueling his growing curiosity and apprehension.

"Step forward, Wolf," Adolam's voice resonated with undeniable authority, compelling Wolf to comply. Reluctantly, he took a hesitant step toward the mysterious archway. Doubt and apprehension swirled within him, urging him to resist this unknown path. "No, forget it," Wolf protested, his voice laced with defiance. However, before he could act upon his hesitation, darkness engulfed his senses. A sudden blow to the back of his head rendered him unconscious.

When Wolf finally regained consciousness, he found himself sprawled upon a bed of rough sand and jagged rocks, positioned at the very edge of a vast lake. "Ah, it's about time you woke up," Silas greeted him, his tone tinged with a mixture of amusement and satisfaction. Rachel loomed over him, an expression of resolute determination etched upon her face. The animosity within Wolf surged, his desire to unleash his wrath upon these individuals intensifying.

Yet, as he rose to his feet, a remarkable sight unfolded before them. The tranquil surface of the lake was suddenly disrupted by intense bubbling and frothing, capturing the attention of all present. Their bickering fell silent as the water began to churn and rise, culminating in the emergence of three majestic beings hovering above the shimmering depths. Their very presence exuded an awe-inspiring power.

In thunderous unison, the ethereal figures questioned the purpose of their summoning. It was Rachel who stepped forward, her voice carrying a mixture of conviction and reverence. "We have brought you the murderer of our pack," she declared, her words directed at the formidable beings.

Amidst the ethereal echoes, the lake gods responded with incredulity. "You are human, you have no pack," they admonished her, dismissing her claim. Unfazed, Rachel pressed on, revealing the source of their transformation. "This is the one you allowed to be human," she proclaimed, her voice trembling slightly. A ripple of amusement emanated from the divine entities. "Who has made you human, little wolf?" they inquired, taunting her with their omniscient knowledge.

Fear etched upon her countenance, Rachel admitted their pact with the swamp hag, the one responsible for their metamorphosis. Her words hung in the air, anticipation mounting as the lake gods considered her revelation. In an enigmatic response, they acknowledged their offering. "So it seems you have. Step forward, Wolf," they commanded, their voices resonating with an undeniable power.

Wolf's defiance burned within him, his resolve hardened against whatever fate these deranged individuals had in store for him. The weight of niceties no longer burdened him; he was prepared to unleash his wrath without reservation. With measured steps, he advanced toward the divine presence of the lake gods.

The gaze of the lake gods bore into Wolf, scrutinizing his every fiber. Their judgment fell upon him, finding him guilty of his crimes, while accepting the grisly gift that Rachel had offered. Unyielding, Wolf locked eyes with the deities, his simmering hatred palpable in the air. As the words of the lake gods echoed through the expanse, a transformative power stirred within him. Rising from the ground, he defied the laws of gravity, hovering above the water's surface.

A swirling vortex materialized beneath him, a testament to the forces at play. Suspended in mid-air, his gaze fixed upon those who stood at the shore, he harbored a burning desire for revenge. At that moment, an unspoken vow passed between them, an unbreakable bond forged in fury and determination. Wolf knew that someday, he would exact his retribution upon those who had brought him to this fate.

Then, with an abrupt shift, the forces of the lake seized him. Like a marionette caught in the throes of a tempest, he was irresistibly drawn into the depths of the water. The churning vortex swallowed him whole, consuming him in its watery embrace. Darkness closed in around him, obscuring his vision and confining him to the mysterious depths of the lake. As Wolf descended through the abyssal depths of the lake, he felt a relentless force pulling him downward, akin to being sucked into the maw of a colossal drain. Swirling currents surrounded him, a whirlwind of water and darkness. In an instant, he was propelled from the depths and expelled into an unknown realm. The place he found himself in bore the unmistakable essence of the swamp—the scent of decay and the clammy touch of wet earth permeated the air.

Shaking off the disorientation, Wolf rose from the murky waters, his drenched form a stark contrast against the dim surroundings. The water's depth at his emergence was shallow, just below knee level, allowing him to regain his footing. Gazing around, he beheld the familiar sight of an untamed swamp. Moss-draped trees towered above him, their gnarled branches reaching out like skeletal fingers. The water, stagnant and dark, held secrets within its depths. It was an eerie and foreboding place.

With no clear destination in mind, Wolf embarked on a purposeful stride through the treacherous terrain. Each step he took sent ripples through the murky waters, disturbing the silence that enveloped the swamp. The squelching of mud beneath his boots became a companion, accompanying him on his solitary journey. His senses heightened, alert to the unseen dangers that lurked in every shadow and thicket.

Amidst the labyrinthine paths, he pressed on, guided by an instinct honed through a life fraught with danger. As Wolf continued his solitary journey through the treacherous swamp, he occasionally caught glimpses of his reflection in the murky waters. However, the image that stared back at him bore little resemblance to the man he knew himself to be. Instead, it mirrored the visage of a majestic wolf, its features distorted by the turbid nature of the swamp's waters. Wolf dismissed it as a mere illusion, a trick of the light and the muddled depths.

Unperturbed by the strange reflection, Wolf trudged onward, his senses acutely attuned to the surrounding environment. It was then that he felt the reverberation of a colossal thud, followed by another and yet another, each growing in intensity. The ground trembled beneath his feet, foretelling the approach of an immense presence hurtling toward him with increasing speed. Though obscured by the dense foliage, Wolf knew something formidable was charging in his direction.

In the face of imminent danger, Wolf steeled himself, cautiously pressing on. His heart pounded with adrenaline, his every instinct urging him to evade the oncoming threat. Suddenly, the monstrous beast crashed through the trees, a nightmarish entity racing directly toward him. Disbelief clouded Wolf's mind, questioning the reality of this grotesque encounter. Yet, as the creature closed in, he had no choice but to act swiftly, determined to ensure his own survival.

Without hesitation, Wolf veered to the side, narrowly escaping the creature's path of destruction. Seizing fallen branches from the swamp-ridden ground, he swiftly broke them, fashioning makeshift weapons. Summoning every ounce of strength and agility, he charged headlong at the beast. In a daring display of bravery, he rolled to the side as the creature lunged, thrusting the sharpened branches into its powerful limbs. Undeterred, he climbed the monstrous form, methodically piercing his way up its body until he reached its colossal neck. With resolute determination, he drove both improvised weapons deep into its flesh.

The creature succumbed to its mortal wounds, crashing heavily to the ground. Wolf dismounted the vanquished behemoth, his heart still pounding from the harrowing encounter. Yet, his relief was short-lived as the enigmatic figure of the swamp hag materialized before him. Her presence filled him with a mixture of confusion and curiosity. "Thank you," she uttered, her voice laden with unexpected gratitude.

Caught off guard, Wolf couldn't help but voice his bewilderment. "He wasn't yours?" he questioned. The swamp hag sighed, her weary eyes meeting his gaze. "No, he was not mine. Those so-called lake gods are nothing but impostors," she replied. Wolf's skepticism deepened, and he pressed for answers. "What do you mean 'so-called'? And why do they seek to keep you here? Aren't you the one responsible for entangling me in this predicament?" he demanded.

With a heavy sigh, the swamp hag divulged the truth, shattering his preconceptions. "Yes, I am responsible for them and all that has transpired. However, those beings masquerading as lake gods are not true deities, for there is only one lake goddess in these realms, and that goddess is me," she confessed, her voice tinged with regret and weariness. Wolf leaned against the massive head of the vanquished beast, his laughter echoing through the desolate swamp. "So, you're the lake goddess, huh? What a turn of events," he jested, unable to contain his incredulity. The goddess met his jest with a somber expression. "Laugh if you must, but it's the truth. I possess little power, and I am imprisoned within these murky confines. I have yet to discover an escape," she revealed, her voice heavy with resignation.

Wolf straightened himself, his curiosity piqued. "You're serious then. Tell me everything," he implored, his tone tinged with newfound determination. The goddess sighed, her gaze fixed on the unfathomable horizon. "I know little of those interlopers who have usurped my realm. They do not belong to any known order or pantheon. Their motives for seizing control, for transforming you into a human, elude me," she admitted, frustration evident in her voice. "I anticipated that your pack would utilize you as a bargaining chip, offering you as payment to secure a false resolution for the transgressions you allegedly committed against them. While these impostor lake gods possess formidable power, their strength lies in their numbers. One alone could have been easily dealt with."

The revelation left Wolf pondering the unknown facets of his existence. "So, you sought me out because you sensed something in me that these beings feared? They wanted to keep me far removed from their realm, even erasing my memories as a wolf. I don't recall my childhood, my family, my past beyond the confines of the club," he confessed, his voice tinged with a hint of sorrow. He gazed into the murky depths beneath him, where the reflection of a wolf stared back. "Is that why I see the image of a wolf when I look into the water?" he inquired, seeking confirmation.

The lake goddess nodded, her expression grave yet filled with understanding. "Indeed, the wolf within you still lingers, a remnant of who you once were. It is a reflection of your true nature," she affirmed. Sensing a newfound resolve in Wolf, she listened intently as he proposed a plan. "If there are two more of these beasts, it is plausible that they guard portals leading out of this forsaken place," he suggested, his mind working through the possibilities. The lake goddess contemplated his words, a faint smile gracing her lips. "Let us investigate, my companion. We shall discover the truth," she declared, her eyes glazed over as she immersed her hands into the murky depths of the swamp, entering a trance-like state.

"I've found them," the lake goddess declared, her voice resonating with a mixture of triumph and urgency. Rising to her feet, she set off with purposeful strides, and Wolf followed in her wake. "They're both in the same location," she informed him, her words driving their determination. Nodding in silent agreement, Wolf pressed on, wading through the treacherous swamp alongside her. The murky waters clung to them, the weight of the stagnant air growing heavier with each step. Yet, undeterred, they persisted.

After what felt like an arduous journey, they reached the designated spot, only to find it seemingly devoid of their quarry. They separated briefly, each scouring the area independently. Lost amidst the strangeness of the swamp, the surroundings appeared increasingly alien to Wolf. Now his primary objective was to reunite with the lake goddess, to find his anchor amidst the disorienting depths. The swamp seemed to thicken, both in substance and atmosphere, its putrid stench permeating the air. Sinister tendrils seemed to slither around his legs, a chilling sensation that failed to hinder his progress. Determined, he pressed onward.

Suddenly, a massive snake emerged from the murky waters, lunging at him with malicious intent. Its coiling tail ensnared his legs, its strength formidable. Wolf grappled with the creature, realizing that mere wrestling would not be enough. A surge of primal rage surged within him, and he unleashed his savage instincts. With relentless fury, he tore into the monstrous snake's throat, rending flesh with his teeth until its resistance waned, succumbing to his relentless assault. Untangling himself from the still-twitching serpent, Wolf found himself faced with two menacing alligators. They lunged at him, jaws snapping with deadly precision, and he engaged them in a brutal struggle. In that intense battle, he tapped into hidden reserves of strength, defying the limits of what he believed possible. Eventually, through sheer determination, he emerged victorious, albeit battered and wounded.

Despite his injuries, Wolf remained undeterred, resuming his quest for the lake goddess. The swamp seemed to darken, ominous shadows engulfing his path, until he arrived at a patch of absolute darkness. Emerging from its depths, the two remaining guardians confronted him, emanating an aura of malevolence and power.

They stood at the precipice of the encompassing darkness, right where Wolf had positioned himself. With a voice oozing with malevolence, one of the guardians taunted him, his words laced with arrogance, "Ah, little man, what do you think you're going to do, eh?" His chilling laughter mingled with that of his companion.

However, while their laughter still echoed through the air, Wolf charged toward them with unyielding determination. But just as he neared his targets, the lake goddess appeared around the bend. Recognizing the urgency of the moment, she mustered every ounce of her dwindling power and unleashed it upon Wolf. In response, he underwent a remarkable transformation, growing in size and stature. As he engaged the beasts in a frenzied clash, he could feel his features shifting, his very essence becoming more primal with each passing moment. Reality blurred, and the line between human and animal blurred alongside it. Before he could fully comprehend the extent of his metamorphosis, he stood above the lifeless bodies of both adversaries. Covered in their blood and wide-eyed with feral intensity, he turned his gaze towards the smiling lake goddess.

"Well, let's find that portal," she said, her voice infused with both satisfaction and purpose. Wolf nodded, his body returning to its original form. "Thanks for your help back there," he acknowledged gratefully. "Of course," she replied, her smile unwavering. "Now, let's continue our search. It must be here somewhere." Wolf pointed towards the impenetrable darkness that had birthed the monstrous creature, convinced that the answers lay within its stygian depths. The part of the swamp where the darkness loomed appeared impervious to any light, an inky blackness that seemed to defy all illumination. The lake goddess acknowledged his intuition with a nod, and together they ventured forth, stepping into the abyss.

In the absence of any discernible sight, they relied on unwavering determination to guide their footsteps deeper into the heart of darkness. Then, a peculiar phenomenon occurred: the darkness itself began to slither and crawl over Wolf's being. It enveloped him, not with a menacing grip, but rather with a touch that felt oddly benign. Sensing the anomaly, Wolf couldn't help but inquire, "Is the darkness embracing you as well?" The lake goddess responded, her voice tinged with curiosity, "No, it's not. And are you certain it's the darkness, indeed?" "Yes, it's touching me, and it is undoubtedly the darkness," Wolf affirmed. "Good," she responded. Perplexed, he questioned the lake goddess, "Good? What do you mean?" A mischievous laughter escaped her lips, her amusement palpable. "Ask it to reveal the location of the portal," she instructed. Wolf complied, and as if the very essence of the darkness seized him, it began to guide him with purposeful intent.

Eventually, their eyes caught sight of a mesmerizing bluish-green glow emanating from a swirling pool ahead. Grateful for the guidance of the darkness, Wolf expressed his gratitude, and it reciprocated with a gentle, lingering embrace. He didn't mind its lingering presence; it felt strangely comforting, like a long-lost comrade.

Curiosity ignited within Wolf as he contemplated their next move. "So, how does this work? Do we simply leap into the pool?" he inquired. The lake goddess offered her insight, her tone laden with certainty. "You can pass through, I believe. However, I, on the other hand, am forbidden. I am certain of my inability to cross over," she admitted. "If, by some means, you manage to vanquish or expel them, I shall finally be liberated," she explained. "You are the chosen one, Wolf. Even the darkness itself has found solace in your presence. Now, go."

"I will return for you," Wolf vowed before plunging into the pool. As he descended into the depths, his strokes transitioning into an upward trajectory, intermittent bursts of radiant light momentarily blinded him. The final burst, however, proved to be the most overwhelming, coinciding with the pivotal moment of inversion. He propelled himself upwards, driven by determination, but the blinding intensity of the breakthrough left him temporarily enveloped in a disorienting white luminescence. In the depths of the pool, Wolf's senses heightened, compensating for his sight's temporary absence. A surge of mounting water pressure engulfed him, its weight bearing down on his being. He sensed a palpable shift in the surroundings, an impending convergence of malevolent forces. Thousands upon thousands of creatures, brought forth by the deceitful lake gods, closed in on him from every conceivable direction.

Just as the horde neared its fateful collision with Wolf, a flicker of vision returned, granting him a fleeting glimpse of the impending onslaught. But before his eyes could fully discern the imminent threat, darkness descended once more, shrouding his world in an abyssal void. In a frenzied display of unrestrained brutality, Wolf tore through the horde with a savage fervor. The world around him transformed into a crimson haze as the darkness clung to his very being, merging with the remnants of power bestowed upon him by the lake goddess. Empowered by this union, he became an unstoppable force, undeterred by the relentless onslaught. Wave after wave of creatures swarmed him, yet he pushed forward unwavering.

The onslaught seemed ceaseless, an unyielding tide that threatened to engulf him. But the darkness and the lake goddess's gift sustained him, defying the boundaries of mortal endurance. Had it not been for the forces at play within him, any ordinary man would have long succumbed to the perils of being submerged underwater for so long.

Finally, with a surge of strength, he broke free from the water's depths, ascending above the surface. Even as he hovered, his wounded body dripping with the evidence of his fierce struggle, the relentless creatures below continued their desperate attempts to drag him back into the watery abyss. His eyes, once human, now held an otherworldly intensity—lifeless yet surging with an overcharged energy.

The false lake gods, witnessing his ascent, initially trembled in the face of his unyielding resolve. But a glimmer of confidence flickered within them, fueled by their belief that they had vanquished the lake goddess and rendered this wolf-turned-man, a mere puppet of their power, incapable of challenging them. Unbeknownst to them, the darkness remained his ally, while traces of the goddess's power still coursed through his veins.

Before the inevitable confrontation could unfold, the waters churned violently, a tempestuous upheaval that heralded the lake goddess's emergence. In the face of her escape, the false lake gods, consumed by fear, took flight, vanishing into the heavens. Wolf grounded himself on the land, his mind still grappling with the mysteries of his transformation. He turned to the lake goddess, seeking answers. "Well, lady, I don't know what that was all about, but are you good?" he inquired, his voice tinged with a mix of confusion and concern. Her smile reassured him. "Yes, I am well, and I owe you my gratitude, Wolf," she replied, her voice carrying a hint of warmth and appreciation.

As Wolf peered into the water, observing his reflection and seeing the visage of a wolf staring back at him, he couldn't help but wonder about his own existence. "They are gone, but why am I still a man?" he pondered aloud, a tinge of frustration creeping into his voice. The lake goddess remained silent, her smile enigmatic, yet comforting.

Shrugging off his lingering questions, Wolf acknowledged the pressing matters at hand. "I have business to take care of," he declared, his voice resolute. With a parting nod, he bid farewell to the lake goddess and embarked on his journey.

Returning to his club, Wolf tended to his wounds with meticulous care. He cleansed and stitched each cut, the physical pain serving as a stark reminder of the emotions boiling within him. A shower washed away the grime of battle, revitalizing him. He nourished his body with a meal, his appetite fueled by an ever-growing rage.

The time for reckoning had come, and Wolf was not going to rely on mere footsteps to reach his destination. Retrieving his rarely used motorcycle from the back, he straddled the powerful machine with a sense of purpose. With each rev of the engine, the fury within him intensified, blending with the growl of the motorcycle.

Arriving at the massive hotel, Wolf gazed up at the towering structure. The voices within him, a chorus of darkness and vengeance, resonated deeply. They egged him on, feeding his determination. Dismounting from the motorcycle, he knew full well that a direct entrance would be denied. Undeterred, he circled around to the back, seeking an alternative route.

To his fortune, a painter's van caught his attention. A worker was in the process of donning a paint suit. Wolf approached him, his eyes filled with an intensity that demanded attention. He offered the painter, a substantial sum of money in exchange for one of the suits. The painter, enticed by the offer, agreed, handing Wolf a suit. Wolf expressed his gratitude to the painter and swiftly donned the paint suit, assimilating into the hustle and bustle of the hotel. The security personnel regarded him with indifference, recognizing him as one of the painters. Within him, a tempest of rage brewed, consuming his thoughts. They had betrayed him and sold him out in a deal that left him as the sacrificial offering. Mistakes may have been made, but their decisions and treachery would not go unpunished. Now, the time had come for retribution.

As the elevator ascended, Wolf's anger intensified, his grip on control slipping with each passing floor. The seething fury within him radiated, amplifying the intensity of his purpose. The elevator dinged, the doors opened, and Wolf stepped out, his gaze fixed on the room doors ahead. With a powerful kick, he sent the doors crashing open, a manifestation of his unyielding determination.

In an instant, all eyes and weapons in the room were trained on him. Rachel and Silas, their expressions etched with horror, stood frozen alongside Adolam. Even the humans clutching their guns trembled in the presence of an indescribable fear. Wolf's appearance was that of a deity, both awe-inspiring and terrifying. His physical form seemed to expand, his aura exuding an ominous darkness. His eyes smoldered with an infernal intensity, commanding attention and submission.

Breaking the stifling silence, Wolf's voice dripped with mockery. "Surprised to see me?" he taunted, edging the terror that gripped the room. Fear consumed them, causing Adolam and Silas to transform into wolves instinctively. The humans, overcome by panic, unleashed a hail of bullets upon Wolf. Yet, their futile attempts merely grazed his flesh, failing to impede his relentless advance. He grew in stature, his very skin appearing ready to burst under the strain. A guttural roar escaped his lips as his face contorted, partially transforming into a fierce wolf-like visage. His eyes blazed a blood-curdling shade of red.

Unyielding and unstoppable, Wolf pressed forward, his path marked by the fallen gunmen. Bullets merely scratched the surface of his formidable being as he marched with unwavering purpose toward Silas and Adolam. The air crackled with raw power, an aura of wrath surrounding him. Silas and Adolam launched themselves at Wolf, their feral instincts taking over. With lightning reflexes, Wolf seized Adolam by his snarling jaws, his fingers finding leverage to tear the predator's maw apart. Simultaneously, Silas clawed at Wolf's arm, but it was a futile attempt. Wolf's strength was unmatched. In a savage display of force, he flung Adolam through the penthouse windows, the shards of glass shattering into a thousand glittering fragments.

Turning his attention to Silas, Wolf grabbed hold of one of his legs, mercilessly ripping it from his body. The grip on his arm weakened, allowing Wolf to seize Silas by the scruff of his neck, delivering a final crushing blow, obliterating the wolf's skull against the unforgiving floor. A chilling silence settled upon the room as the remnants of Silas and Adolam lay lifeless, their former companions rendered speechless.

"My quarrel is not with you, men. I seek Rachel. Where is she?" Wolf's voice, laced with a dangerous calm, reverberated through the room. One of the survivors, with trembling resolve, stepped forward to answer. "She escaped as soon as she had the chance, sir. We do not know her whereabouts," he admitted. Wolf surveyed the room, studying the bewildered faces of those who remained. They were oblivious to Rachel's true nature and motives. He knew he had to find her, and he sought an escape route.

Spotting a door, Wolf swiftly made his exit, navigating through the winding corridors. However, just as he descended the stairs, a heavy blow struck him from behind, sending him tumbling down to the first landing. His vision blurred momentarily, but when clarity returned, Rachel loomed over him, her presence casting a dark shadow. Wolf met her gaze, struggling to rise to his feet, when suddenly, everything faded into darkness.

As consciousness resurfaced, Wolf found himself overlooking the vast expanse of the lake. The self-proclaimed lake gods hovered before him, their ethereal forms suspended in the air. A profound unease settled within him. Something felt off, his very being transformed. He felt smaller, distorted. Wolf turned his attention to the lake's reflection, where the visage of a wolf stared back at him. Briefly, the illusion of his human facade flickered before dissolving into the unyielding gaze of a wolf. Some realizations washed over him.

Slowly turning around, Wolf discovered a pack of wolves behind him. His eyes met Rachel's, as well as those of Silas, Adolam, and the others. And amidst the pack, the wolves he had once fed poison, or had he? The weight of his actions bore heavily upon him. With a snarl contorting his face, Wolf turned his attention back to the false lake gods. "What say you, do you wish to be human," the lake gods demanded. Their deceit now laid bare. In a display of primal fury, Wolf lunged at them with every ounce of his being. Claw and fang tore into their flesh, as he unleashed a relentless assault. Amidst the chaos, the water surrounding them began to convulse, churning with an ominous energy. The once serene surface transformed into a tempestuous maelstrom, swirling with crimson currents of blood-stained foam.

Emerging from the tumultuous depths, the true lake goddess manifested in all her resplendent glory. Radiating power and authority, she commanded the false deities to retreat. Hastily, they ascended skyward. Wolf, relinquishing his grasp, plunged into the water, resurfacing near the safety of the shore. As he stood on solid ground once more, he turned to behold the lake goddess, her smile a testament to her approval. It became evident that she had orchestrated the vision of his humanity.

Now, it was time to face the wolves that had betrayed him, or had they? It didn't happen, but it would have. They made him look like a betrayer, but he didn't poison his pack, they just wanted him laden with guilt so he would feel like he deserved punishment. With an unwavering determination, Wolf unleashed his fury upon Rachel, Silas, Adolam, and the others who had stood by their treachery. Their lives were extinguished one by one, their betrayal met with the savage justice of their leader. The remaining wolves, though bewildered, placed their trust in Wolf's judgment.

Amidst the aftermath, a voice resonated across the expanse, offering Wolf a choice. "Do you wish to be human?" The lake goddess's question hung in the air, tempting him with the allure of humanity. Yet, as the echoes reverberated, Wolf let out a mournful howl, a proclamation of what he is, a wolf.

Spheres of Confinement

Max had been asleep for hours when a frantic tapping on his window jolted him awake. Groggy, he stumbled over and slid the window open, already knowing who it was. Only one person ever showed up at such odd hours—Reid. As the window creaked up, Reid was already halfway inside, babbling incoherently, words spilling out too fast for Max to catch.

"Slow down," Max mumbled, rubbing his eyes.

"I've got it, Max! They're coming—you've got to hide me," Reid said, his voice tinged with desperation.

"Got what?" Max asked, still half-asleep.

"No time to explain! We need to go, now!" Reid yelled, panic in his eyes.

A loud thud echoed from upstairs. "Great, you woke up my roommate," Max groaned. "He's insane."

Reid let out a dry laugh. "You think he's crazy? Stick around a few more seconds, and you'll see real crazy."

As soon as he said it, multiple beams of light cut across Max's backyard, all converging on the window. Then came the unmistakable sound of heavy footsteps approaching—fast.

"What the hell is happening?" Max asked, turning to Reid.

"No time!" Reid shouted, grabbing Max by the shirt. They crashed through the door just as the window shattered and gas canisters were lobbed inside. Max barely glimpsed figures in the chaos as Reid yanked him up the stairs.

Reid kicked open Max's roommate's door. The guy barely had time to stand up before Reid pointed at him. "You've got two choices: run with us or face what's coming. Your call."

Without waiting for a reply, Reid rushed toward the back of the room. "Max, is it still here? Is it still here?"

"Yeah, yeah, it's over there," Max said, pointing to a worn panel in the wall.

Reid tore it away and grinned. "Perfect. Let's go!"

Max's roommate, now fully on board, followed close behind as they slipped into the hidden passage. Max quickly sealed the entrance the best he could. Years ago, he had installed a handle on the inside, a way to escape and be alone, but he had nearly forgotten about the maze since taking on a roommate.

They navigated through the dark, twisting passages until they reached a small door.

"This is it, right?" Reid asked, a hint of uncertainty in his voice.

"Yeah, it should open," Max replied.

Reid gave it a hard pull, and the door creaked open. The three of them crawled through, only to find themselves in a strange, unexpected place—a museum-like room filled with old, dusty artifacts.

Max stared, bewildered. He knew nothing about what lay before him, but Reid's eyes lit up. This was his world.

Reid spun toward Max, eyes wide with urgency. "Max, is there another way out? We need to move. Now."

He reached for the small door, but before his hand could touch it, a steel wall slammed down, obliterating the door with a deafening crash. The three men exchanged tense glances.

"What the hell have you gotten me into?" Max's roommate, Ted, shouted.

"Shut up, Ted," Reid snapped. "We've got bigger problems."

A cold, steady voice echoed from the dark corridor. "Yes, you do."

Footsteps, slow and deliberate, approached from the shadows. Max's heart raced. "What do we do?"

Reid grinned, almost too calmly. "Wait."

The footsteps grew louder, then a figure stepped into the dim light—a tall, imposing man with a chiseled jaw, a perfectly trimmed white beard, and eyes that were both warm and terrifying. His presence radiated authority, making Max feel like a child in front of a school principal. And when he spoke, it was with a calmness that masked a fury, like the eye of a storm.

"Reid," the man said, his voice smooth but laced with menace. "You have something that belongs to me."

Max felt a chill crawl up his spine. "Reid, just give it to him. Let's get out of here."

Reid smirked, shaking his head. "You really think it's that simple, Max? We're not going anywhere."

Ted, looking panicked, raised his hands. "Hey, I don't know what's going on here. I just want to go home. Can we do that?"

The man's lips curled into a smile. "Oh, Ted, I'm sure you know nothing. I'll have someone escort you and Max home."

A clean-shaven, muscular man in a tailored suit stepped forward, motioning for Ted and Max to follow. Max glanced at Reid, who shook his head slightly, signaling not to go.

"Wait," Max blurted out. "What if Reid gives you back whatever it is he took, and we all leave together?"

The man turned his piercing gaze toward Reid. "Well, Reid? What do you say?"

With a sigh, Reid reached inside his coat and pulled out a small box, its surface gleaming with red jasper. He handed it to the enigmatic figure.

The man smiled, a predatory gleam in his eyes. "Well then, I suppose you're free to go."

Max let out a sigh of relief. "See, Reid? Let's just get out of here."

But the man's voice cut through the moment like a knife. "Did you open it, Reid?"

"No," Reid replied, a hint of defiance in his tone.

The man's eyes twinkled with a dangerous curiosity. "Would you like to?"

Reid's smirk returned. "What do you think?"

The man chuckled, a low, unsettling sound. "Follow me, gentlemen."

Reid followed immediately, while Max and Ted hesitated, needing a shove from the imposing men flanking them to move forward. Max's mind raced as they walked through dimly lit corridors, each lined with strange adornments and unsettling sights. What had Reid dragged them into? The deeper they went, the more surreal it all became. Max just wanted to be home, far away from whatever nightmare this was.

Eventually, they entered a massive chamber with towering 30-foot ceilings. Four monstrous gargoyles loomed in what would have been the corners, if the room even had corners. Twelve colossal pillars lined the walls, and in the center of the room was a strange, intricate mechanism that looked like a chaotic tangle of gears and metal. Max couldn't even begin to guess its purpose.

"Come closer, but don't enter the circle," the enigmatic man instructed, his voice calm but commanding.

They gathered at the edge of the circle while the man stepped inside. He turned to face Reid. "This is what you stole, Reid. Did you even realize what you had?"

He opened the red jasper box, and as he did, the area within the circle lit up, bright as the sun but oddly gentle on the eyes. Max squinted, trying to comprehend what he was seeing.

"Look closely, Reid," the man said, pulling a glowing, crystal-clear sphere from the box. "This is far more valuable than money, young man."

He placed the sphere onto one of the mechanisms, then walked to a panel on the side and flicked a switch. Instantly, a pure beam of light shot up from the floor and struck the sphere. The man calmly stepped out of the circle, and as he did, the space inside the circle exploded into a dazzling display of colors and dimensions. It was as if reality itself was bending, revealing sights Max couldn't have imagined.

But something felt off. Despite its magnificence, it seemed incomplete.

"This," the man said, his voice cutting through the visual chaos, "is just one-third of the puzzle. I need two more spheres like this."

He turned off the switch, and the lights dimmed as the covers slowly slid back over the sphere. With a wave of his hand, the man gestured for his men to round them up. "I've decided to alter my plans. Instead of dealing with this myself, you three are going to help me find the other two spheres."

Max's stomach churned as they were led into another vast room, this one cluttered with stacks of manuscripts, books, and massive rolls of paper scattered across the floor. Every inch of wall space was covered with maps and screens, making the room feel like some kind of madman's war room. Two men sat silently at computers, not even glancing up as they entered.

In the center was a large table, and the enigmatic man motioned for them to sit. Once they were seated, he began to speak.

"My name is Renald Sterling, and I'm a collector of sorts," he said smoothly. "However, my position was not gained through collecting alone. That's a story for another time if fate permits. For now, let's focus on the task at hand."

"I and my team have been searching for the other two for a very long time. And now, it seems we might have a lead on one," Renald said, his voice smooth and calculated. "This is where you come in, Reid—and your friends." He gestured casually toward Max and Ted, as if they were mere accessories to Reid's role.

Reid frowned. "What are you talking about?"

Renald smiled, a knowing grin. "You're a good thief, Reid. Had you stolen from anyone else, you would've gotten away clean. But I was waiting for you."

Reid's eyes narrowed. "Waiting? What do you mean?"

"You don't steal junk, Reid. You knew exactly what you were taking, or you wouldn't have bothered," Renald replied, his tone measured. Reid leaned back, saying nothing. Renald's smile widened. "Ah, I see. Well, let me ask—do you know where the others might be?"

Reid shifted in his seat. "I thought you said you'd found one?"

"We have. But confirmation is always useful, and don't forget—there's still one more out there. So, do you?" Renald asked again, his gaze unwavering.

Reid hesitated for a moment before answering. "Let's just say one is in the water, and the other... is in the sky."

Renald nodded, sitting back in his chair. "Good. We've already located the one in the water." He turned toward the men at the computers. "You hear that?"

"Yes, sir. We're on it," one of them responded without turning from the screen.

Meanwhile, Ted was trembling. He had always tried to act tough around Max and Reid, but he'd never been in anything remotely like this. The tension was crushing him.

"Boss, this guy hasn't stopped shaking," one of Renald's men commented, pointing at Ted.

"Give him a trank. That should calm him down," Renald ordered.

One of the men retrieved a pill from a small bottle, handing it to Ted along with a bottle of water. "Here, take this. It'll help."

Ted glanced at Max and Reid, who just shrugged. With no other choice, Ted downed the pill and took a gulp of water, hoping for some relief.

Renald clapped his hands lightly. "Alright, boys. Let's get moving."

"Where are we going?" Reid asked, though he already seemed to know the answer.

Renald shot him a sharp look. "You know where, Reid. Stop pretending."

With that, they were herded toward the exit, once again following Renald's lead. Outside, a sleek limo waited for them. Renald and his men spoke quietly among themselves as the others sat in tense silence, wondering what lay ahead.

Max was utterly lost, overwhelmed by everything unfolding around him. The pill they'd given Ted had taken effect, and he was no longer trembling, but that didn't ease Max's growing anxiety. After being driven to a private airport, they boarded a plane and took off. Hours later, they landed as the last slivers of daylight vanished from the sky.

Upon arrival, they were whisked into another car and driven to an isolated spot, far from any signs of life. When they finally stopped, Renald stepped out with a grand flourish. "Here we are, boys," he announced, spreading his arms wide like a showman unveiling his masterpiece.

His men didn't need orders. They immediately shoved Reid, Max, and Ted toward a waiting boat. Renald hopped in after them, taking the helm. He fired up the engine and laughed, pushing the throttle forward as the boat cut across the dark water.

At one point, the authorities appeared alongside them. Max's heart skipped—maybe this was their chance for rescue. But the men aboard simply nodded at Renald, waved, and disappeared into the night. Clearly, the authorities weren't on their side.

After about 40 minutes of speeding across the water, Renald eased up on the throttle and brought the boat to a stop. His men rose from their seats, calmly retrieving diving gear. Without a word, they began suiting up Max, Reid, and Ted.

"Any of you know how to dive?" Renald asked, almost casually.

"No, I don't," Max admitted, panic creeping into his voice.

Renald glanced at him, a twisted smile forming on his lips. "Oh well. You were going to die anyway."

Max's eyes widened. "Wait, what? You're kidding, right?"

Renald didn't answer, just continued staring at Max with that unsettling grin. Max's heart pounded in his chest as he looked over at Reid. "Man, do you know how to do this?"

Reid nodded. "Yeah, I do. Just follow my lead, you'll be fine."

Max wasn't convinced. "What about Ted? He looks totally out of it."

Reid gave him a grim look. "I don't think they care, Max. Not about us. Not about him."

Max swallowed hard, nodding. He glanced over at Ted, who was barely coherent, slouched and vacant-eyed.

Renald approached the three of them, his voice calm and cold. "Alright, boys. Here's the plan..."

Renald had laid out the plan. It seemed straightforward enough, but with the darkness and the depth of the water, things felt far from simple—especially with only one of them knowing how to dive. Despite their reservations, the time came. They were handed lights and gear and told to get in the water. Reid went first, slipping in smoothly, while Max and Ted hesitated on deck, unsure. It didn't take long before they were shoved in after him.

Max immediately panicked as the cold, black water enveloped him. He flailed for a moment until Reid surfaced nearby. "Hey, buddy, it's okay. Just breathe," Reid's voice came through the earpiece, steady and reassuring. Ted swam up sluggishly, his movements slow and uncoordinated, but he didn't seem to be in a full-blown panic.

"Follow me," Reid instructed. Max and Ted nodded, trailing behind him into the abyss. Max was overwhelmed; he could only see what his light touched, and he kept it trained on Reid, his only point of reference in the endless black. Ted swam beside him, quiet but present.

They dove deeper and deeper until they entered an underwater cave. Max's anxiety spiked as they wound through the narrow passageways. Suddenly, Reid stopped ahead of them, and Max froze. His earpiece crackled to life with Reid's panicked voice.

"Stop! Go back! Now! Leave—quick! I don't know what it is, but get out, fast!"

Before Max could react, Reid swam past him in a flash, but Ted was gone—he wasn't beside him anymore. Max tried to move, but something held him fast. He thrashed, struggling to break free, but it was no use. He was being pulled deeper into the cave, and terror gripped him.

Max's heart raced as he fought against the invisible force dragging him away. Suddenly, Reid's light cut through the water, illuminating him. Reid swam back toward Max, ready to strike at whatever had him. But just as Reid was about to attack, Max felt a massive jolt surge through his body. His entire frame lit up, then plunged into darkness as he lost consciousness.

Reid still struck at the creature—a tentacle-like appendage that had wrapped around Max—but it had already released him, retreating into the black. Wasting no time, Reid grabbed Max's limp body and pulled him toward the surface.

By the time they broke through the water, Ted was already in the boat with Renald's men. Reid shouted for help, his voice desperate. "Get him in! Help me get him up!"

The men scrambled, reaching down to drag Max out of the water and onto the deck. Reid followed, panting from the effort.

"What the hell was down there? Renald—my friend is dead!" Reid yelled, his voice thick with panic and anger.

Renald, calm as ever, stroked his chin, staring down at Max's still body. "Hmm," he muttered, his expression unreadable.

"Why didn't I think of this sooner?" Renald muttered.

"Think of what?" Reid asked, still in shock.

"That you were better off dead than alive this whole time," Renald replied coldly. Without hesitation, he pulled out his phone and started giving orders. Within minutes, a patrol boat pulled alongside theirs. Renald climbed aboard.

"Throw the body in here," he ordered, and his men followed without question, tossing Max's lifeless form onto the patrol boat. "One of you come with me," Renald continued. "The rest of you wait here with these two. We'll be back in two hours."

Reid stood frozen, unable to comprehend what was happening as Renald's boat sped away into the dark waters, disappearing into the black void of the night. They reached Renald's plane swiftly and, after a short flight, returned to his secluded mansion. The men carried Max's body into the room with the twelve towering columns and the intricate mechanisms in the center.

"Lay him down in the circle," Renald instructed, his voice measured. He opened the jasper box, revealing the glowing sphere within. Placing it into its cradle, Renald and his companion made sure to step outside the circle before Renald prepared to activate the mechanism.

But just before he flicked the switch, something stopped him. His face flashed with realization.

"No," Renald said aloud, his hand pausing mid-motion. "No, I almost made a huge mistake. I would've incinerated the body."

He strode over to Max, pulling a massive blade from his coat. With one swift motion, he drove the blade into Max's chest and sliced downward, exposing his lifeless heart. Renald reached into the cavity, extracted Max's heart, and turned back to the glowing sphere. He removed it from its cradle, sliced open the heart, and placed the sphere inside it.

With deliberate precision, Renald placed the heart back inside Max's body, then returned to the edge of the circle. He exchanged a knowing smile with the other man in the room and finally flicked the switch.

Instantly, the space inside the circle exploded into a storm of light and energy. Lightning-like streaks of geometric shapes twisted and morphed into something incomprehensible, expanding and contracting, threatening to tear through the boundary of the circle. Renald and his companion instinctively stepped back, watching the spectacle unfold.

Amidst the chaos, Max's still figure began to stir. Slowly, he rose to his feet, his body glowing a molten orange that shifted to a cold, steel blue. His movements were deliberate, his form now radiating with an otherworldly power. Yet, as Max reached the edge of the circle, he paused.

He couldn't pass.

Renald flicked off the machine, and the swirling lights vanished. Max could now cross the circle's edge—but he didn't. He stood there, staring blankly at Renald, motionless.

"He's mine now," Renald said, smiling darkly. "My slave warrior. As long as I wear this," he held up a pendant around his neck, "he's bound to me. He'll retrieve the other spheres—he's connected to them now. I should have thought of this sooner. It would've saved us a lot of time and money."

Renald turned to his companion. "Shall we?"

The other man nodded, and they boarded the plane, bringing the reanimated Max with them. After a short flight, they met up with the boat where they had left Reid and Ted. As they pulled alongside, Reid stared in disbelief at Max, while Ted, lost and confused, still hadn't grasped the full horror of what had happened.

"What did you do to him?" Reid demanded, his voice tense.

Renald waved his hand dismissively. "Relax, Reid. I've improved your friend. And honestly, you and your quivering pal there are no longer necessary."

Max stood before them, transformed—his skin a dark, shifting gray, veins of glowing orange pulsing beneath the surface. His eyes were a strange, piercing blue, and his hair had taken on an even darker shade of black-gray. His body was marred with scars, sealed over but permanent, remnants of the energy that had torn through him during his reanimation. But most unnerving of all was the absence in Max's expression. His face was void of emotion, his mind seemingly empty.

Renald chuckled. "As a matter of fact, boys—you know what to do."

Without hesitation, his men grabbed Reid and Ted, dragging them toward the edge of the boat. Despite Reid's protests and shouts, they tossed both of them overboard.

"If you survive, good for you. If not—oh well," Renald called after them, his voice casual and uncaring.

He then turned his attention back to Max, rubbing the pendant around his neck. "Go get it, Max," he commanded.

Max's cold, glowing eyes met Renald's. There was no hesitation. He nodded once, like a beast obeying its master, and dove into the water. The moment he hit the surface, something deep within the depths triggered a response—not Max's original mind, but a new one. Something primal.

Max sliced through the water effortlessly, his body moving with an unnatural grace as he navigated the caves, each twist and turn bringing him closer to his target. As he approached, a voice began to echo in his mind, resonating through the stillness of the deep.

"We are the same. They are using you. You will be extinguished."

The voice was calm but urgent. Yet Max felt nothing in response—not fear, not doubt, just the cold emptiness that had consumed him since his transformation. He pressed on, unaffected, focused only on his mission.

The creature guarding the sphere loomed before him, a massive beast with a single glaring eye, its tentacles writhing in every direction. It unleashed a barrage of dark, oozing darts, which sliced through the water and tore into Max's body. He barely registered the impacts—no pain, just the sensation of the hits, dull thuds and zings. His eyes remained fixed ahead, razor-sharp and unblinking.

He pushed through the storm of tentacles and darts, unrelenting. The beast lashed out, but Max tore through its defenses, plummeting directly into its eye. Tentacles coiled around him, trying to pull him back, but he ripped his way through the creature's head, carving a path toward the radiant glow of the orb buried deep within.

As his hand reached out to claim it, the voice returned, echoing more urgently now.

"This is a mistake."

But the warning fell on deaf ears. Max yanked the orb from its cradle, and the colossal creature went limp, its body collapsing around him. With the sphere in hand, Max swam out of the beast's lifeless form and navigated his way back through the caves, indifferent to the destruction he had wrought.

He emerged from the water, dripping but unscathed, and handed the sphere to Renald, who burst into laughter.

"Ahahaha! Well done, Max! Better than I could've hoped!" Renald's grin stretched wide as he eyed the glowing orb, then glanced at Max. "But look at you... What the hell happened down there?"

Max's voice was strained, robotic, as if forming words had become an effort. "I got the sphere."

Renald's grin widened. "That you did. Now, we've got one more to find. Max—do you know where it is?"

Without warning, a surge of energy exploded through Max's mind, igniting his senses. His consciousness expanded in every direction, seeing through vast distances and gathering visions of far-off places. The energy coalesced, drawing him to a single location. His mission became clear.

"Yes," Max said, his voice flat. "I know where the other sphere is."

Renald clapped his hands together, ecstatic. "Perfect! Let's head back, secure this one, and get ready for the next. What do you say, Max?"

Emotionless, Max gave a single nod. Renald turned to his men, barking orders.

"Boys, let's move!"

And with that, they sped off into the night, the hunt for the final sphere already underway.

Once back at Renald's estate, the sphere was quickly secured as he wasted no time preparing for the next excursion. Max revealed the location of the final sphere, unaware that once they claimed it, he would be the next to fall.

"We're heading to the City of Bones," Max said in his emotionless tone.

Renald's brow furrowed. "City of Bones... but not the one you're thinking of, boys. From what I can see, it's going to be a tough journey." He paused, rubbing his chin. "But... I might have a plan."

He stepped away to make a phone call. Minutes later, he returned, a twisted smile on his face.

"Alright, we can land at a small airstrip near our destination. I've arranged for jeeps to take us the rest of the way, so maybe it won't be so bad after all. Let's move."

They gathered their gear and departed. The flight went smoothly, as did the initial travel through the outskirts of the city. Their journey led them to a barren place, marked only by an ancient ring of stones, seemingly forgotten by time.

Renald stepped out of the jeep and surveyed the area. "Where's the entrance?" he muttered, growing impatient.

Max stood still, his eyes scanning the stones. "It's not seen with eyes," he replied cryptically.

Renald shot him a frustrated glance. "Keep looking. There has to be a way in."

Max suddenly raised a hand. "Stop. Close your eyes, all of you," he commanded.

Reluctantly, the men obeyed. As their eyes shut, an odd sensation filled the air, like a shift in reality itself. Max lifted his face toward the sky, his eyes absorbing the light of the sun. His gaze ignited like twin suns, casting an eerie glow over the surrounding blackness that had crept in unnoticed. Slowly, Max turned his eyes downward and began to spin. As he did, the light and darkness spiraled around him, and the ground beneath their feet started to heave and ripple as though alive.

"Open your eyes," Max said.

When they did, they were surrounded by thick darkness, but before them lay a staircase—an ethereal spiral made of smoke, constantly shifting and alive. The men exchanged uneasy glances, the surreal scene before them. The darkness seemed confined to the stone formation, shrouding the area in an unnatural gloom.

Max gestured to the staircase, signaling Renald to descend, but Renald, always cautious, motioned for Max to go first.

The descent was strange, as if the staircase wasn't solid at all. Every step felt unstable, like walking on air that could give way at any moment. Yet, Max moved effortlessly, gliding downward as though the stairs were as firm as stone under his feet, while the others followed behind with far less certainty, bracing themselves with each step as they ventured into the unknown.

Once they reached the bottom, the staircase of smoke retracted into nothingness, leaving no trace of their passage. Dim light seemed to emanate from the bones themselves, casting eerie shadows on the group. As their eyes adjusted, they realized they were standing on massive skeletal remains—the walls, ceiling, and floor were all formed from enormous bones, far too large to be human.

Max began to walk forward, unfazed, while the others stood in awe. The entire labyrinth was composed of these colossal bones, each corridor and chamber stretching out in a macabre display. Gold adorned the upper bones, glinting faintly in the dim light, and even the bones near the ceiling had a silver sheen as though they had been dipped in precious metals.

One of Renald's men whistled softly. "Boss, that's a fortune in gold up there. What do you think?"

Renald shook his head. "No, what we're after is worth far more than any gold or silver. Don't lose focus."

The group pressed on until they came upon a massive gate, constructed entirely of bones and encrusted with jewels. An ominous sign hung from the gate, etched with the words: *Pass not to the other side of this gate.*

Without hesitation, Max unlatched the gate and stepped through. As soon as he crossed to the other side, he vanished from sight.

The men exchanged nervous glances. One of them turned to Renald. "Sir, should we follow him? We have no idea what's beyond that gate, but he survived the water alone. Maybe he'll be fine here, too?"

Renald pondered for a moment, stroking the pendant on his chain with a smug expression. "No need. we'll wait for him to return. He can't go anywhere I don't want him to. Not as long as I have this."

The men seemed to relax at his words, comforted by the fact that Max was still under Renald's control and that they didn't have to follow him in past the gate.

Meanwhile, Max wasn't aware that he had vanished. All he noticed was that his surroundings had changed drastically. The world beyond the gate was different—darker, older, and filled with an overwhelming sense of power.

The energy within Max surged, instincts kicking in as he whirled around just in time to see three immense, twisted figures lunging at him. Without a thought, he let his body take over, moving with unnatural precision and power. Had he been human, he might have noticed that these creatures were far from ordinary. They flickered in and out of existence, but every time they reappeared, Max was there, striking with brutal force until they disintegrated into dust—or something resembling it.

With the strange beings vanquished, Max continued onward, following the inexplicable pull inside him. He turned a corner and found himself facing two towering knights, their bodies ablaze with roaring fire. They stood like sentinels, their molten eyes fixed on him.

"You may not pass," they said in unison, their voices like crackling embers.

Max paused, but only for a moment. His body responded to the challenge. His hair ignited, flames flickering where strands had once been, and his skin darkened, hardening into something like coal. His eyes blazed with a cold, blue-white flame. Without a word, he lowered his head and marched forward.

The fire knights crossed their battle axes in front of him, barring his path. A twisted grin spread across Max's face. The thought of battle seemed to stir something primal in him, charging him with even more energy. In one swift motion, he grabbed both axes, twisted them inward, and drove them into the fiery heads of the knights. They staggered back, their flames flickering violently, but Max didn't pause to finish them off. He walked straight through the opening they had tried to block, feeling only the faintest twinge of curiosity about why he hadn't crushed them completely. It didn't matter—he kept moving.

As Max pressed on, strange beings of mist and shadow began to swirl around him in a frenzied storm, their forms darting past him without making contact. The swarm thickened, the air growing darker and heavier until everything around him was pitch black. Yet still, Max walked, unperturbed.

Then, suddenly, he felt nothing beneath his feet. The swarm vanished, and Max found himself suspended in a vast, star-filled void. It looked like space, though he wasn't certain. In the center of this cosmic expanse, an epic, god-like being hovered, its gaze locked on Max.

"A husk," the being's voice echoed with a mix of curiosity and ancient power. "I haven't seen a husk in millennia. What is your name, husk? Or are you still not truly conscious?"

Max tried to focus, his mind a fog of half-formed thoughts, but nothing connected.

"Ah, I see. Let me help you," the being said, raising a hand. Max's mind ignited with clarity, though it still felt foreign—like a puzzle with pieces missing, replaced by something else, something...new.

"You're being controlled, aren't you? A husk like you can be bound by a particular kind of amulet." The being's words struck deep.

"I have to take it," Max said, his voice steady but hollow, as if the words were not entirely his own.

"I know," the being replied calmly. "But did you realize, husk, that I am the original keeper of the sphere you now seek? None have taken it from me in eons. The one you've already stolen—he was ancient and mighty. And the one that resides within you...was once held by the mightiest of us all."

Max's eyes flickered with something—awareness, confusion—but the being continued.

"How the third was taken remains a mystery, even to me. How it was hidden from me is equally intriguing," the being mused, its gaze narrowing. "The machine they've built, it meddles in things none of them can comprehend. They think they understand power, money...but these relics were not meant for men. Their purpose has long been forgotten, but there was a reason we were chosen to guard them."

Max stood still, absorbing the ancient one's words.

"You are a husk," the being repeated, its voice thick with realization. "They didn't consider this." With that, it shifted into a shimmering vapor and flowed into Max, entering through his nose.

Now the voice wasn't external—it was inside him. A cold whisper in his mind. "Look in your hand," it said.

Max glanced down, and there it was—the sphere.

"Let's go back and see what they'll do," the voice inside Max whispered, calm but calculating. Max nodded, turned, and retraced his steps past the fire knights and through the gate. In an instant, he reappeared before Renald and his men.

"Ah, there you are," Renald greeted him with a sly smile. "You made it. Now, hand it over."

Max held out the sphere, but as Renald reached for it, Max didn't let go immediately. He tightened his grip, his cold eyes locking with Renald's. "Are you sure you know what you're doing?" Max asked, his voice steady but more human than it had been since his reanimation.

Renald faltered, surprised. Max had barely spoken a word since being brought back to life, but now, there was something different in his gaze—something questioning, maybe even resisting. Renald quickly recovered, forcing a smile as he pulled the sphere from Max's grasp. "Yes," he said, his voice firm. "I know exactly what I'm doing."

With the sphere in hand, Renald turned on his heel. "Let's go," he ordered. They returned to his mansion, where everything had begun. The group funneled into the grand room dominated by the strange machine. Renald placed the sphere in its cradle beside the other one, stepping out of the circle and positioning himself in front of Max with a smug grin.

"Well, my friend," Renald said, his tone almost mocking, "it seems our time together has come to an end. I'd like to thank you for your service."

Max barely had time to react before a sharp, blunt pressure struck his neck. He felt something—something more than the numbness he'd known since being reanimated. It was the spirit of the ancient being that had shared his body, now forcing its way out, pouring from his mouth like smoke and reforming beside Renald.

"It's time we take that sphere back now," the spirit said, its voice cold and merciless.

Max's mind flickered—suddenly lucid. Awareness hit him like a wave, but it was too late. His body convulsed as he heaved, a violent retching overtaking him. He could feel the sphere inside his chest, the one tied to his very life, start to move, pulling free from its place in his heart. An intense orange glow spread across his chest, growing brighter with every passing second.

For the first time since his reanimation, Max felt pain—unimaginable, soul-crushing pain. The agony ripped through him, as if his entire body was being torn apart from the inside out. His once-numb senses now screamed in torment, every nerve alight with unbearable suffering. It was like being plunged into hell, or at least something damn close to it.

Max tried to speak, to form words, but the pain stole his voice. He could only gasp and choke as his body fought against the inevitable. Renald and his men stood back, watching with cold fascination, waiting for the prize to emerge from his broken body.

Max's mind began to blur, his thoughts warping like a fevered dream. His vision darkened, reality twisting around him as the agony consumed everything.

Suddenly, a shadow darted from the corner, smashing into the machine with a thunderous crash. Renald, the spirit being, and his men spun around in shock, only to face a monstrous, grotesque creature tearing through the machine like it was nothing. With a deafening roar, the beast snatched the two spheres from their cradles, crushing the machine in the process.

The spirit being grinned, a sinister smile curling on its ethereal face. "Oh, Reid... You were told never to transform again. Have you forgotten so soon?" it taunted.

"Reid?" Renald stammered, eyes wide with disbelief. "That's Reid? What... what is he?"

The spirit chuckled darkly, casting a disdainful glance at the towering beast. "He's a hybrid. A hybrid of what, you ask?" It sneered, shaking its head. "No one remembers anymore. His family committed atrocities that defy memory. Who knows what lives within him? He could carry the essence of sixty different supernatural beings... or more."

Renald's face paled as he took a step back. Meanwhile, Max lay crumpled on the floor, writhing in agony as the sphere within him crawled closer to his throat, burning with every movement. His body convulsed, each second more unbearable than the last.

With a guttural growl, Reid spoke, his voice like gravel scraping against stone. "I have both spheres. Even yours," he said, his voice dripping with menace.

Renald's men opened fire, filling the air with the roar of gunshots as they unleashed a hail of bullets upon Reid. But the bullets had no effect, merely bouncing off his thick, monstrous hide. Reid let out a feral snarl, leaping from the circle and cutting down Renald's men with brutal efficiency. Heads rolled, bodies crumpled to the ground—within seconds, all that remained was a bloodstained room, Renald standing alone and the spirit at his side.

Through the haze of searing pain, Max's vision flickered, catching glimpses of the towering beast. For a moment, amidst the chaos and torment, a strange realization struck him—this monstrous creature was on his side.

Max's breath hitched as the sphere continued to tear through him, his vision blurring again, but not before he saw the beasts blazing eyes settle on Renald. Then the beast turned into Reid, but Max could barely make sense of it through his blistering pain. He tried to rub the crust from his eyes, but his skin was searing—flaking off in brittle patches, locking up in places until it cracked. His mind, only partly his own, spiraled with confusion. How did Reid even get here?

Before he could grasp an answer, the spirit being materialized, its form twisting into something solid, and with a sneering grin, it hoisted Max from the ground by the back of his neck. "We have your friend... and the last sphere," it chuckled, a cruel laugh reverberating through the air.

Reid, unphased, stared back coldly. "He's not my friend anymore, and as for the sphere—what do you think you're going to do with just one?" His voice was laced with disdain.

As the spirit being shook Max's body, it triggered something deep inside—the sphere lodged within him suddenly stopped its agonizing movement and began to spread. It pulsed, expanding like wildfire into every part of him. Max's body, once crumbling and broken, stiffened with an unnatural force.

"So, you think you're some kind of king now, Aloria?" Max's voice was different, deeper, a menacing growl that seemed to scrape out from the depths of his soul.

The spirit being froze, its mocking grin faltering as it dropped Max instantly. "How... how do you know my name?" it stammered.

Max landed on his feet with a thud, now standing tall, his eyes locked on the being. His presence was different, far more commanding. "Do you not remember a true king, Aloria? Has it been so long?" His voice was steady, laced with an authority that sent chills through the room. "And who has dared to hold my power all this time?" His gaze shifted to Renald, who, sensing the shift, nervously clutched the pendant hanging from his neck.

Renald's smirk wavered as he stroked the pendant. "It worked on Max... I controlled him easily enough," he muttered, voice unsteady.

Max—or whatever now possessed him—chuckled darkly, stepping forward with slow, deliberate strides. "That may have worked on the shell, but me? No, little man," he sneered. "Your attempts to play the king... laughable."

Max's newfound power rippled through the room as he approached Renald, an ominous presence, ready to reclaim what had been his all along.

Reid and the other being in the room could only watch, frozen as the entity now controlling Max commanded an aura of absolute authority. The air itself seemed to hum with power as Max stood before

Renald, who frantically rubbed his amulet, his panic growing more feverish with each passing second. But the more Renald stroked the amulet, the weaker he became. His strength drained, his posture crumbled, and soon, he was on his knees before Max, trembling.

"You've given me a conduit to take your life," Max—or rather, the entity—said, voice deep and cold. With a slow, deliberate breath, he inhaled, and wisps of glowing green smoke were pulled from Renald's body, swirling into Max's mouth. As the light was drawn from him, Renald's skin turned a sickly gray, then began to flake away, crumbling into ash that scattered at Max's feet.

Max turned his gaze to Aloria, his voice seething with accusation. "You have betrayed your vows, your birthright—your king."

Aloria, eyes burning with defiance, scoffed. "You, my king? We were equals once, Inglious. How did you come to wear the crown? By storming through and taking it! And Inglious, how did you become a keeper of the spheres? You think it was an honor?" He sneered, venom in every word. "It wasn't for your might or your glory. They hid you from the rest of us, locked you away. The wars, the laws you built—they've all been forgotten. No one remembers you now... except me."

A twisted smile curled at the corners of Max's—Inglious's—lips. "Your fear betrays you, old friend," he said, voice low and mocking. "The desperation in your words fouls the very air you breathe."

Aloria's defiance wavered for just a moment, his twisted smile faltering as the weight of Inglious's presence bore down on him. The room felt suffocating, and it became clear that the balance of power had irreversibly shifted.

Aloria's words had barely escaped his lips when he attempted to phase away, but Max's hand clamped around his throat with ruthless precision.

"Leaving so soon, old friend?" Max's voice carried a mocking edge as he smiled down at Aloria. "But then again, you're no longer the keeper of your sphere. That role belongs to the hybrid now." His grip tightened, fingers digging in. "So, tell me, Aloria... what should I do with you?"

A heavy silence fell. Then, with a sharp toss, Max threw Aloria to the ground. "Go," he commanded coldly, "do as you will. But if I ever see you again, it won't end well."

As the final words left Max's mouth, Aloria vanished.

Max turned to Reid, who still held the two spheres, his form now shifting back to human once again. "And now... what to do with you, hybrid?" Max said, eyeing Reid intently.

Reid met his gaze, calm yet resolute. "My name is Reid," he replied, holding up the spheres. "I'll give you both if it means I get my friend back."

Inglious, now inhabiting Max's reanimated body, fixed a reflective gaze on Reid. His thoughts spiraled inward, questioning how he had been pulled back to the sphere he had once failed to protect. He had lost it, been destroyed—or so he'd believed. Was it this husk of a body that had called him back upon reanimation? His eyes remained locked on Reid, though his vision seemed to drift far beyond the present moment.

Reid stood in tense silence, observing the conflict playing out across Max's altered features. He had a chance to flee, but that wouldn't help him save his friend. Finally, Inglious spoke, his voice weighted with centuries of regret and contemplation.

"What are you planning to do with them?" Inglious asked.

Reid hesitated, shifting his grip on the orbs. "I don't know," he admitted. "All I knew was that Renald had some sinister plans, and I couldn't let that happen."

Inglious's eyes narrowed. "Do you even comprehend what you hold in your hands, hybrid?"

Reid glanced down at the spheres, their energy pulsing faintly. "I know what they are, and I understand their danger," he replied. "But as for what comes next... I'm uncertain. My grandfather had told me some stuff. He was my guide in everything supernatural and strange. We only started discussing the spheres a month ago, so my knowledge is incomplete. But I know they can't fall into the wrong hands."

He looked up at Inglious, curiosity mixed with caution. "If I may ask—without offense—how could someone like you have ever been a keeper of such power?"

Inglious sighed, the weariness of eons etched into his expression. "I had reached the apex of power in my realm," he explained. "But over countless ages, I grew... not bored, but deeply discontented. The spheres were forged to contain evil realms so twisted they shattered laws across every realm, even your own. I took on the role of keeper to find meaning, but it was never a simple task. I paid dearly for my failures, just as I still bear the weight of them now."

"I relinquished my kingdom to lesser beings," Inglious said, his voice carrying the weight of ancient regret. "Yet it mattered little to me. My reign had become meaningless. If I could at least prevent this wicked power from spreading across all things, perhaps I could redeem myself." His eyes grew distant as he continued, "But the memory of how I lost the sphere eludes me. All I know is that it was stolen, and I was scattered across the realms, never meant to return. Somehow, though, your friend's reanimation with the very sphere I guarded has pulled me back into existence."

As Inglious spoke, something began to shift. The sphere that had embedded itself within Max's body started to move, inching upward until it slipped from his mouth, hovering in the air between them. The energy of the sphere pulsed, and Inglious's essence began to separate from Max. Like an ethereal tide, the essence was drawn out and coalesced around the hovering sphere, forming a tangible, fearsome figure.

Max's body crumpled to the ground, lifeless once again. Reid rushed to his fallen friend, his face contorted with desperation. He turned toward the fully manifested Inglious, whose form radiated the aura of a monstrous, warrior king. Despite his dread, Reid spoke with defiance. "Can you help me, or do I smash these spheres right now?"

Inglious regarded Reid with a calculating gaze, his presence as formidable as the stories of ancient legends. "Put one of the other spheres into his chest," he said, finally. "It might work."

Reid hesitated, realizing that Inglious hadn't truly answered his question. He had no guarantee this would save Max, but if the sphere that once reanimated his friend could do so, perhaps one of the others would have the same power. What neither of them knew was that the sphere Inglious had once guarded had become intertwined with his emotions—his remorse, his desire to set things right. That twisted, ancient power had grown to share Inglious's yearning for redemption, creating a unique bond. The other spheres, however, harbored no such transformation. They remained cold and unfeeling. Reid pressed one of the spheres into Max's chest, hoping desperately for a miracle. The absence of Renald's strange machine seemed insignificant now—perhaps it had only been used to control Max. Reid didn't know. All he knew was that the moment the sphere entered Max's chest, his friend bolted upright, eyes wide and gleaming. Yet something about those eyes seemed off, like a puzzle with pieces just barely misaligned.

He reached down, helping Max to his feet, and turned to Inglious. "He won't really be himself, will he?" Reid asked, worry lacing his voice.

Inglious shrugged, the movement almost casual for a being so ancient and imposing. "Hard to say," he replied. "While I inhabited his body, pieces of Max remained intact. But there was also the sphere's influence and Renald's control. I wish I could tell you more, but matters of the human spirit and reanimation weren't exactly my specialty. I was a keeper, not an expert, just a vessel to protect."

Max placed a reassuring hand on Reid's shoulder. "I'm fine, old friend," he said, voice steady. "It's me." Reid searched Max's face, noticing how his friend's eyes now looked familiar, his skin gradually returning to a healthier hue. Relief washed over him.

"Good," Reid said, still cautious. "But you do realize that something else is keeping you alive now, right?"

Max nodded, a small smile playing at his lips. "I do. And I also know you're not exactly human," he said, his voice softer but firm. Reid's eyes narrowed, tilting his head in surprise. "How do you—?"

Inglious interjected with a dismissive wave. "He'll have scattered memories, Reid. He saw you change."

Reid sighed, resigned. "Yeah, I'm what they call a hybrid," he admitted.

"A hybrid of what?" Max asked, curiosity lighting his face.

Inglious groaned, clearly annoyed. "Do we really have time for this?" he snapped.

Reid shot him a look. "Yes, we do," he replied. "Why don't you make yourself useful and search the house? Maybe you can figure out what Renald and your friend Aloria were plotting."

Inglious, the towering warrior king, gave a grin that was more unsettling than comforting before he strode out of the room, leaving Reid and Max alone. Reid let out a breath and turned back to Max, his expression thoughtful. "Honestly," Reid began, "I'm not even sure what I am anymore. My family lineage stretches back millennia, tangled up with all sorts of supernatural beings."

Max's brows furrowed, but he listened as Reid continued, his voice drifting into an almost story-like rhythm. "It all started with my great-great—ten times great—grandmother. She lived deep in the forest, a widow while still young. After her husband died, she chose isolation. She had everything she needed: food, water, shelter, weapons. But loneliness settled in, and though she hated going to town and found the people there strange and off-putting, she spoke to the forest to ease her solitude. She'd talk to the trees, the birds, anything that would listen.

"One day, she felt eyes on her while she wandered the woods. She turned and saw something—a figure—watching her from the shadows. But before she could get a better look, it vanished. She called out, inviting it back, but the forest swallowed her words, and she saw nothing more. When she returned home, though, a massive bouquet of wildflowers waited for her on the doorstep. She was delighted.

"Every day after that, a new bouquet appeared. Long story short, this... being eventually revealed itself, and, well, they fell in love. They married, had children. But when the townsfolk found out about her unusual husband, they threw curses and malice their way, driving them deeper into the woods. The marriage was strange, yes, but it drew the curiosity of even stranger beings who started mingling and leaving their marks on our bloodline.

"So, generation after generation, more and more supernatural entities added their essence to the family. Creatures from realms most people wouldn't dare imagine. Now," Reid finished with a sigh, "I'm this bizarre cocktail of beings. A hybrid of so many things that even I have no idea what I am."

"My parents gave me up for adoption," Reid said quietly, "hoping I'd bring the human bloodline back. They never liked being... beasts. They wanted to be normal, to leave that part of our heritage behind. They figured if they sent me away, I might live a human life, untouched by the transformations that haunted them." He shook his head. "But they were wrong. The change still came, no matter how much they wished otherwise."

Reid's expression softened as he continued, "Luckily, my grandpa would visit me, telling me stories about our family's history and why I was different. Even then, I managed to live a pretty normal life— then you and I became friends. Being around you made me feel even more human. But then I heard about the spheres and Renald's schemes, and everything changed. No one really knows the full extent of what these spheres are capable of, but whatever dark power is locked inside them can't be good."

Max's face lit up with a strange, almost mischievous smile. "Well, looks like we're both a little different now," he said, and for a moment, the tension seemed to ease.

Just then, Inglious burst into the room, his massive form barreling through the doorway. "Are you two done yet?" he bellowed. "I found something. Look at this." He marched over, clutching a handful of ancient, weathered manuscripts.

Reid peered at the papers. "This looks old," Inglious declared with pride.

"Can you read it?" Reid asked, a flicker of hope in his voice.

"No," Inglious admitted gruffly.

Max raised an eyebrow, smirking. "Then how do you know it's old?"

Inglious glared at Max, clearly unamused. "Because I can feel its age, *monkey*," Inglious snapped, the last word laced with a hint of disdain. "Aloria must have stolen this. But from whom? And even if he did, he couldn't have read it himself. He doesn't know this language."

"Could he have learned?" Max asked, a hint of worry in his voice.

"No," Inglious said firmly. "This language is reserved for the Etheric Seers. And they don't share their knowledge lightly. They won't see just anyone either. It's sacrilege even to try and force them. They're revered across realms, even by me. I gave them sanctuary, a place of their choosing, so they wouldn't have to hide in remote places." His voice softened, touched with an old reverence. "We need to arrange a meeting with the Etheric Seers."

"How do we do that?" Reid asked, frowning. "You said they don't see anyone."

Inglious's eyes narrowed. "No, they don't. But they will see me."

He cast a sideways glance at Max, a look of unease creeping across his mighty features. "What about your friend?" he asked, nodding toward Max. "He still doesn't look right."

"I'm fine, really," Max insisted. "How do we do this meeting? And hold on, I've got to ask—why are we even doing all this? We have all three spheres. We're good, aren't we?" He looked between Reid and Inglious, a hopeful smile cracking his tired features.

Reid and Inglious exchanged a grim look before Reid spoke. "Technically, yeah, we have them. But Aloria had a plan, and he's still out there. We can't assume we're safe just because we've got the spheres."

Max shrugged, still clinging to his optimism. "How do we know he'll actually do something crazy? Why not just wait for him to come to us?" He paused, his smile widening. "Besides, he'd have to destroy you, me, and then get through Reid to get what he wants. Our bases are covered, don't you think?"

Inglious clenched his jaw, his patience thinning. "What about the scroll?" Reid interjected, trying to regain focus.

Max waved his hand dismissively. "It was probably just used to locate the spheres. What else would it be for? It can't have anything to do with Aloria's bigger plan."

Frustration etched deep into Inglious's expression. He held up the ancient scroll, eyes burning with determination. "I still need to know," he said. "I'll find the Seers. See you later."

"No, wait!" Reid protested, his voice cracking with alarm. "We shouldn't separate!"

But Inglious was already moving, his massive form fading into the shadows of the room.

Inglious let out a short, mocking laugh. "I won't be long, *hybrid*," he said, the insult barely disguised.

"It's Reid," he called back, but Inglious had already vanished, leaving them in an uneasy silence.

Reid turned to Max with a forced grin. "Well, old friend, any ideas on how we pass the time while we wait to get attacked?" he joked.

Max's smile was thin, almost cold. "For starters, let's get out of this room. Maybe head to the sitting area. Our host isn't coming back," he said flatly.

Reid blinked, caught off guard by Max's uncharacteristic chill. But he brushed it off, chalking it up to the strain of everything they'd endured. Together, they moved to the opulent sitting room, where massive, inviting chairs and elegant couches awaited. The room was lined with ornate mirrors, rich wood tables, and a well-stocked bar gleaming in the corner. They settled in with a drink, trying to regain some sense of normalcy amidst the chaos.

Meanwhile, Inglious materialized in the hallowed chamber of the Etheric Seers. The room, once bright with ethereal light, felt fractured and wrong. Only six of the twelve seers were present, each seated in their appointed places, shadows darkening their usually serene features.

"What is this?" Inglious thundered, his voice filling the chamber. "Where are the others?"

The six seers rose, their movements slow and burdened. They bowed deeply before him, their voices trembling. "Oh great warrior king, ruler of the times of plenty and safety," one of them intoned. "We have fallen into the darkest time of our existence."

Before the king could respond, one of the seers collapsed forward, his hands striking the ground. The earth beneath him splintered, and he began to convulse, gray-black smoke pouring from his mouth, sinking into the cracked earth below. The other seers and Inglious watched in horror, frozen with helplessness as the dark magic consumed their companion. The ground swallowed the smoke and the broken man's body, leaving nothing but a groaning scar in the earth.

One of the remaining seers, his voice heavy with desperation, spoke. "They have cursed our realms, oh king. We need your strength once more, your rule, your justice of iron and mercy."

Inglious clenched his fists, old oaths stirring within him. "Sit with me," he commanded, his tone softened but resolute. "Tell me everything."

The seers gathered around him, recounting the terrors that had befallen the realms since he had been sealed away as the sphere's keeper.

"The sons of Koraal ruled in your stead," one of the Etheric Seers began, their voice heavy with the weight of centuries. "They ruled as one but were divided in all things. Even the fate of the spheres and our continued existence became points of contention."

Inglious listened, his massive form tense with restrained anger as the seer continued. "One brother decreed that the spheres should be released back into their realms but bound by strict barriers, unable to freely traverse between worlds. His vision was one of control, of order maintained through separation. The other, wanting to be seen as magnanimous, declared that the spheres should return to their original glory. He argued that the eons of imprisonment had served as just punishment and that their existence was a natural force—one that brought balance and meaning to the chaos. 'Why deny them their nature?' he asked. 'Their inclinations ripple through the realms, shaping order from disorder.'

"These arguments shook the very foundations of the realms," the seer continued, sorrow etching every word. "Many grieved, for neither solution showed promise. Yet others took these debates as permission for rebellion, unleashing lawlessness not seen since the first great upheavals. Reverence for our kind has crumbled. We are mocked, considered relics of a bygone age, and now we are hunted—victims of soul eaters that prey on our kind. Only we five now remain, all that is left of the twelve."

Inglious's heart grew heavy with grief, each revelation a hammer blow. He had been led to believe he was a monster, a tyrant, but he realized now he had been the balance, the bringer of order in a world teetering toward chaos. The truth stoked something deep within him, a power that had lain dormant for far too long. It stirred, rising and surging like an ancient storm, filling him with purpose.

Inglious had held onto a fragment of his former strength, a ghostly echo of the power he once wielded. But now, as the weight of grief and purpose surged through him, his power awakened fully, flooding back with a force he hadn't felt in ages. The sphere embedded within him shattered, and its energy—an entire realm's essence—wove seamlessly into his being. A voice echoed within him, a cacophony of a million souls speaking as one: *We are you now. Nothing can separate us. You are the Warrior King, and we surrender ourselves. Our transgressions have been many, but as we dwelt within you, we transformed. It is our honor to aid you in reclaiming your kingdom.*

Inglious had not considered returning to his kingdom. His exile had been long, and he had resigned himself to his fate. Yet witnessing the devastation wrought by those who sought only power made his path clear. The realms had now descended into chaos, clawing for dominance and destabilizing everything in their pursuit of a crown that meant nothing without wisdom. *There is more to the throne than power,* he thought, his resolve hardening. *Only the small-minded crave to be king. Some of us must bear that burden, not for glory, but because we have to.*

Meanwhile, in the sitting room, Reid and Max shared a few drinks. The warmth of the fire and the effects of the alcohol soon had Reid drifting off to sleep. As soon as Reid's breathing deepened, Max's expression changed. He gently took the sphere from Reid's grasp and slipped away, moving quietly through the corridors until he reached the room where the machine once stood in a circle of etched symbols. Though the machine lay in pieces, shattered by Reid's earlier rampage, the circle itself remained intact—perfect for his needs.

Max stepped into the circle, and the orb he held began to glow, mirroring the one embedded in his chest. As both spheres pulsed with energy, Max tilted his head back, and a light streamed from his eyes and mouth, his voice resonating across dimensions until it reached Aloria. "I have two of the three spheres," Max intoned, his voice both his own and something far more. "And I possess a vessel. Open a doorway for me, now. Quickly."

A shimmering, ethereal portal materialized before him, swirling and beckoning. Max stepped through, leaving the echoes of his departure hanging heavy in the air.

Inglious fixed his blazing, eternal gaze on the Etheric Seers, his presence commanding and unyielding. "I brought this for you to interpret," he declared, handing over the scroll. One of the seers carefully unraveled it, examining the ancient symbols etched in an unfamiliar script.

"Great King," the seer intoned, his voice lined with apprehension. "This scroll is a map to the spheres... and a guide on how to destroy you."

Inglious's expression darkened. "Who wrote this?" he demanded.

The seer's eyes clouded with unease. "We cannot say, O King, nor when it was written. The language is one of the oldest, spoken only in the age of the ancients. Its origin is... peculiar."

Inglious fell silent, his mind churning through possibilities. But before he could dwell on it further, the ground beneath them began to quake violently. One of the seers collapsed, clutching his chest as fissures split the earth around him. The stone groaned, and the familiar, terrible sensation of energy being siphoned away filled the air.

Not this time, Inglious resolved.

Without hesitation, he strode to the widening chasm and leapt into the darkness. The air roared around him as he fell, but he wasn't descending passively. He was a force of fury, plummeting with unrestrained momentum. Power pulsed from his core, defiant and unstoppable.

As he descended, his presence erupted into a swarm of spectral forms, millions of spirits emerging from him, surging ahead to confront the entity below. The soul eater writhed in terror as the spirits assaulted it, harrowing its dark essence before Inglious even touched the bottom. By the time he landed, the soul eater was cornered, writhing and desperate, trying to escape.

A laugh burst from Inglious, echoing through the depths, deep and confident. At the sound, the spirits halted, retracting back into his form, leaving him face-to-face with the terrified creature.

Inglious approached the soul eater, towering over it. "You had a choice," he rumbled, voice resonating with the force of his fury. "This was the path you chose, and now I make mine."

With a single, devastating motion, he swung his arm down. His blow struck with the force of a god, obliterating the soul eater into nothing but dissipating shadows.

Inglious was taken aback, momentarily stunned by the surge of power he now felt coursing through him—greater than ever before. He had not anticipated this. His power had been a fraction of its former self, yet now it was something far beyond.

Without hesitation, he propelled himself upwards, flying through the air like a comet. His speed was unstoppable, his energy now boundless. When he reached the top, he glanced at the Etheric Seers to see if the five remained, and indeed, they were still there, unwavering.

"Well, that one shouldn't trouble you anymore," Inglious said, a slight smirk pulling at his lips. "I'm not sure how many more of those creatures there are."

The Seers smiled with reverence. "Oh, Great King, may we bless you for your triumph?" one of them asked, voice full of awe.

Inglious shrugged. "Sure," he said, unsure of what to expect.

The Seers circled him, their movements synchronized as they threw a handful of shimmering gold dust into the air, mixed with the rarest gem ground to powder. This gem, they explained, could only be found in one place across the realms. As they chanted in their ancient tongue, Inglious felt a shift in the very air around him. He was lifted into the air, surrounded by a swirling green energy that pulsed and writhed like a living thing.

The energy shifted in shape and hue, shifting from green to golden, then to a bright, almost blinding white. It crackled and popped, its form constantly changing until it finally split apart, revealing Inglious standing beneath it, unharmed and stronger than ever. He gently touched the ground as his feet met it once more, the power coursing through him with an intensity he had not known before.

"I don't know what you guys did, but... wow," Inglious marveled, his voice tinged with awe. "I need to get back, but we'll talk later."

With a final nod, he left the Seers and flew off toward Renald's mansion.

Upon his arrival, he found Reid still asleep, sprawled out on the couch. Inglious called out in a booming voice, "Where's the other one?"

Reid shot up, startled, his eyes wide. "What? I—I don't know. I fell asleep. I thought he'd do the same," he stammered, looking around the room frantically.

Inglious chuckled, shaking his head. "Oh, mixed one," he said with a grin. "He doesn't need to sleep. Have you forgotten?"

Both Inglious and Reid searched the mansion, their eyes scanning every corner, but the Max was nowhere to be found. The sense of unease grew between them as they realized that Max was not in the house.

They found themselves standing in the room with the strange machine and the circle. The air felt heavy, tinged with an odd scent that Reid couldn't quite place. "It smells... funny in here," he said, scrunching his nose.

Inglious gave him a knowing glance. "Good nose, ya. That smell? That's a portal scent, my friend. And I'm betting your friend went through it. He must have taken the other sphere since you don't have it, and I haven't seen it or sensed it," he said.

Reid froze. In the chaos, he'd completely forgotten about the sphere. Had Max taken it and left? The confusion swirled around him. He couldn't make sense of it.

Without wasting another moment, Inglious grabbed Reid by the arm. "You're coming with me."

In an instant, they were gone, transported to the realm of the Etheric Seers.

Reid had heard stories about the Seers, but he never imagined he'd find himself standing before them. He expected grandeur, wisdom, something awe-inspiring. Instead, the Seers looked worn, drab, their robes hanging loosely from gaunt, pallid figures. They no longer seemed to carry the aura of ancient power he'd imagined.

Inglious didn't waste time. "Aloria has the other two spheres," he declared, his voice a low rumble.

The Seers' expressions twisted into grotesque smiles. With an eerie, unified hiss, they replied, "We know, oh great king. That was... and that will never be."

Then, the transformation began. Their bodies stretched unnaturally, limbs elongating, faces contorting into monstrous shapes, eyes wild with madness. The grotesque figures moved closer to them, their smiles now twisted into demonic grins.

"These are not the Seers you've heard about, Reid," Inglious said, his voice tinged with grim recognition. "They are no longer themselves. Something has overtaken them. And my fear is they've learned how to destroy me."

As if on cue, the voices inside him spoke, their power lacing through his thoughts. *No, my king. Those tricks will not work on you anymore. With your power restored, and with ours, plus the blessings you've received, those methods will not harm you this time.*

Despite that, a part of him still hesitated. He didn't want to hurt the Seers. They were, after all, the keepers of ancient knowledge, the last remnants of a once-great order.

But the grotesque creatures were advancing, their limbs writhing toward him with predatory intent. Reid, too, seemed to sense the danger. His body began to shift, transforming into something monstrous, his muscles rippling with unnatural strength. He moved to strike.

Inglious raised his hand, stopping him. "We can't hurt them, Reid," he said, his voice firm. The power within him burned, but there was still a thread of reverence that he wasn't ready to sever. Not yet.

Reid hesitated, eyes filled with confusion and anger. But the energy around them was thickening, and the time to act quickly was slipping away.

"What now?" Reid yelled, his voice tinged with frustration as the monstrous Seers closed in on them.

Inglious didn't hesitate. With a powerful stomp of his foot, the ground trembled beneath them. Cracks appeared in the earth, widening into a massive cavern. With swift precision, Inglious gathered the approaching creatures and hurled them into the abyss below. The ground sealed shut behind them, trapping whatever horrors lingered in the dark.

"That should buy us some time," Inglious muttered to himself, scanning the surroundings. "But now... who do we see?"

Reid, ever the pragmatist, suggested, "Why don't we go see the king? Maybe he'll know something."

Inglious shot him a sharp glare. "You mean *the* kings? The ones who rule as one? They're bad news, Reid," he growled, his tone colder than the cavern beneath them. He paused, contemplating. "But... you might be right. It's worth a shot. Good idea. Let's go see them."

Reid hesitated. "Can we just do that?"

Inglious's eyes sparkled with a dark amusement. "Doesn't really matter, does it? We're going anyway." He laid a hand on Reid's shoulder, and without another word, the world around them shifted.

They reappeared moments later before an imposing palace. Towering spires pierced the sky, and the air was thick with a sense of power and ancient authority.

Two guards at the gate eyed them warily. "State your purpose," one demanded.

Inglious grinned, his expression filled with confidence. "We've come to speak with the Kings Koraal."

The guard raised an eyebrow. "And who should I say you are?"

Inglious's smile never faltered. "Tell them... Inglious and a hybrid are here to see them."

The guard's demeanor shifted. He trembled at the mention of Inglious's name, though he sneered at Reid. With a huff, he turned and sent a fiery bird soaring into the distance. Moments later, it returned with a message.

"He's waiting," the guard announced, stepping aside.

Inglious nodded and began walking down the path toward the palace, his stride purposeful. Reid followed, trying to take in the surroundings. He was stunned by the sheer magnificence of the palace—its towering spires, the intricate carvings on every wall, the lush gardens brimming with strange, otherworldly creatures. Exotic beings moved through the halls, their eyes gleaming with the knowledge of centuries.

When they arrived at the court yard, the doors swung open with a low creak. They were announced, and the heavy scent of incense filled the air as they stepped inside.

Reid couldn't help but be awestruck. The court yard was vast, its walls stretching high into shadowed heights. Golden banners hung like rippling rivers of light, and at the far end, two thrones rested, side by side, dark figures seated upon them. Their eyes locked onto Inglious as they entered.

This was no ordinary meeting.

When Inglious entered, the reaction was immediate—a collective gasp rippled through the room. Whispers traveled like wildfire, igniting the air with disbelief.

"I heard you were no more, Inglious," one of the kings mused aloud, his voice a mixture of awe and derision. "The longest-ruling king since anyone can remember, now standing before me. How... interesting, brother."

"Very interesting, indeed," the other replied, eyeing Inglious with a mixture of confusion and disdain. "How can this be? It must be a ghost... or our sources have failed us."

Inglious stepped forward, his voice cutting through their banter like a blade. "Enough of the theatrics. Aloria has two of the spheres. He can't get the third, but what he holds might be enough to crumble all the kingdoms—including yours—and forge a new one with him as its lord. What say you?"

The brothers exchanged a look, their initial surprise quickly turning into mockery. One of them laughed, the sound cold and dismissive. "No one can take our kingdom, Inglious. No one. We command the greatest armies across all realms," he said, his confidence dripping with arrogance. "Aloria will not dare to challenge us."

"And what of my armies?" Inglious's voice was low, steady, but the weight of it hung heavy in the air.

The brothers' faces hardened, their sneers twisting into something darker. "Your armies were dismantled. Their loyalty was only to you," one of them replied, his tone mocking. "They're scattered across the realms. Some completely destroyed. The Colossuses are our armies now—unbeatable, invincible. Who could possibly stand against them?"

Inglious could feel the old fury stirring deep within him. The rage that had once shaped kingdoms and crushed enemies alike. "Bring out your army," he said, his voice thick with menace. "And I will show you how frail you truly are."

The air grew tense. One of the brothers raised a hand, his voice ringing with authority. "So be it. But no powers may be used," he declared, his eyes narrowing as he gestured to the back of the room.

A heavy silence fell, and then—like shadows coalescing into form—six colossal figures emerged from the darkness. Their enormous, hulking bodies loomed, eyes burning with rage. They were giants, titans of unimaginable strength. They towered over Inglious, their presence suffocating, their power almost palpable.

Inglious turned to Reid, his eyes glinting with unspoken resolve. "Step back, kid," he said, his voice calm but carrying an edge of finality.

Reid stared at him, unsure. "Are you sure?" he asked, his voice laced with concern.

"Yeah, I'm sure," Inglious replied with a faint, almost imperceptible smile. His gaze hardened, and he turned his attention fully to the challenge ahead.

The colossal figures closed in, surrounding him like a ring of iron. But Inglious remained unfazed, stepping forward into the center of the ring. He knew what was coming. And then, in the blink of an eye, the battle erupted.

Reid could hardly track the movement. The Colossuses were so massive that they blocked every angle of the fight, their enormous bodies filling the space with crushing weight. But Inglious moved with a grace that defied his size, his movements swift and precise, like a storm tearing through a battlefield. Each strike, each movement was a blur—until, one by one, the Colossuses began to fall.

The ground shook as one of them crumpled to the floor, its body hitting the ground with a deafening thud. Another was sent flying, its massive frame crashing against the court yard walls. The air was thick with dust and the echoes of battle, but all Reid could see were the Colossuses falling—each one, one after another—like giants toppling under the weight of their own arrogance.

Inglious stood in the center, unshaken, his eyes burning with the fury of a king long forgotten. The battle had only just begun, but already, it was clear: no force could stand against him—not even the greatest armies of the realms.

The Colossuses continued to rise, only to be hammered back down or tossed aside with brutal force. Inglious moved with precision, his strikes relentless, each one sending a giant crashing to the ground. But his gaze never wavered from the brother kings, who watched with increasingly distorted expressions of anger.

"Is this enough to convince you?" Inglious bellowed, his voice shaking the walls of the court yard.

The brothers, their faces contorted with fury, shouted in unison. "Destroy him!"

With a cold, calculated calmness, Inglious faced the next approaching giant. This time, there was no hesitation. The moment the Colossus reached him, Inglious detached its head, his powerful foot crushing it beneath his heel. The next giant lunged at him, only to be impaled by Inglious, his body thrusting through the creature like a spear. One after another, they fell—each Colossus torn apart by the sheer might of Inglious's fury.

The room fell silent as Inglious stood amidst the carnage, blood soaking his form. He stared at the brothers, his voice a booming echo that reverberated through the halls. "What say ye now?" His words were so charged with power that they forced the brothers back into their thrones, the sheer force of his presence overwhelming them.

For a long moment, the brothers recovered their composure. When they rose, their voices were laced with contempt. "Oh foolish king who once was," one sneered, "six of our best mean nothing. What army do you have now, fallen king? You cannot stand against us."

Inglious sighed, his eyes hardening. "I am here to warn you of the coming doom, you fools," he said, his tone as cold as steel.

"Ha! From you?" The other brother spat, mocking him.

Inglious's gaze grew distant, almost sorrowful. "How are you kings? What have we become?"

Infuriated, the brothers summoned their entire armies. The ground shook as legions of warriors poured into the court yard, their roar echoing through the chamber. But Inglious remained calm, his voice cutting through the chaos. "Enough."

In a flash, he grabbed Reid by the arm, and in an instant, they were gone—leaving the brother kings to stare, helpless, at the empty space where their enemy had been.

Max appeared in the hidden dimension of Aloria, a place where the very air seemed to hum with strange energy. The world around him twisted in ways that defied logic, its shifting landscapes an eerie reminder of the power that resided here.

Max held out the sphere. "Here," he said, handing it over to Aloria. "This is what you wanted."

Aloria took it with a slow, deliberate movement. "Good. Now, how do you plan to open the one inside the boy so I can harness its power?" he asked, his eyes glinting with hunger.

Max didn't hesitate. "Take the sphere, absorb it, and start there," he instructed, his voice steady.

Aloria absorbed the sphere into his chest, feeling its power surge through him. He trembled with anticipation, but before he could fully comprehend the depth of what he had just done, Max approached him. With a swift, unexpected motion, Max thrust his hand up to chest height and pushed Aloria hard, sending him stumbling backward.

Aloria gasped, eyes wide with panic. "What did you do? What did you do to me?" His voice cracked with rising terror. "I can feel them inside me—" His body writhed as he screamed, "Aaaahhh! Get them out of me! Get them out!"

Max stood back, grinning darkly, his laughter cutting through the chaos. "You wanted it, didn't you? Feels good, doesn't it?" he taunted, his voice dripping with malicious delight.

"No! Nooooo!" Aloria's voice turned shrill with fear. "I'm scared!" His final words echoed as he convulsed, his body beginning to unravel under the immense pressure of the tormented entities now inside him. With a horrific cry, Aloria's spirit exploded, his form bursting apart into a thousand fragments, his essence ripped away into nothingness. The twisted power that had consumed him rushed into Max, surging through him in a violent wave.

Max stood still for a moment, feeling the power swell within him. He was no longer just himself. He was brimming with raw, uncontainable strength. *That weak, sniveling creature... Like we would let him be king,* the millions of voices inside him mocked. *We are the ones calling the shots now. No one is putting us away.* The laughter that followed reverberated in Max's mind, an endless cacophony of triumph.

No sooner had Inglious and Reid left the kings and their armies than Max appeared in the court yard with a twisted, gory grin plastered across his face. "Can anyone join this party?" he asked with mocking cheer.

The brothers turned, their eyes narrowing as they took in the sight of this unexpected intruder. "Who are you? And how did you get in here? No magic can enter unless through the gate. Again, I ask—how are you here, and who are you?" One of the brothers demanded, his voice growing sharp with suspicion.

Max didn't answer. He merely smiled wider, his eyes glinting with dangerous amusement.

"Show this imbecile his way out, men!" one of the brothers commanded, motioning to their remaining forces.

The soldiers, still in the room, began to move toward Max with grim determination. But Max didn't flinch. He calmly walked toward them, his pace unhurried. When they reached him, they attacked—surging forward with fists and weapons raised. They pummeled him, driving him to the ground with brutal force, their strikes relentless.

But Max didn't fight back. He lay there, absorbing every blow, his grin never fading, as if the beating were nothing more than an afterthought.

Max shattered into a thousand fragmented pieces, each one violently torn apart by the raw power. A strange greenish aura flickered around the broken remnants of his body, swirling like a toxic fog. Then, with an explosive burst of emerald light, the pieces gathered together, compressing into a single concentrated point before detonating in a violent eruption.

The energy that followed was unlike anything seen before—a tidal wave of malevolent power, as the countless beings trapped within the two imprisoned spheres surged into the courtyard, spilling forth like a swarm of nightmares. The once-proud armies of the Koraal brothers stood no chance against the onslaught. Screams filled the air as soldiers were torn apart, their frantic strikes swiping at phantom foes, helpless against the invisible force ripping through them.

The kings, who had watched from their thrones, were frozen in horror as their mighty forces were decimated in mere moments. The battlefield became a maelstrom of destruction, a nightmare unfolding in real-time. The air was thick with the cries of the dying, the sound of metal scraping against nothing, as the kingdom itself seemed to crumble under the weight of the invisible storm.

When the last of the armies had been laid to waste, the two realms—separated by time and space—began to converge once more. The shattered remnants of Max's body reassembled, pulled back together by forces unseen, until he stood tall before the Koraal brothers. His form now radiated with an unearthly glow, and the air around him thrummed with power.

One of the brothers, his face pale with disbelief, stammered, "How could this have happened? We had put in safeties... we had prepared for everything!"

Max's voice echoed in a chorus of a million voices, each one laced with venom. "There is always a work around," he hissed, the words crawling through the air like serpents. "I am that work around."

The brothers stood in stunned silence, unable to comprehend what had just unfolded. Their kingdom was in ruins, their armies vanquished, their power stripped away in the blink of an eye.

Max's smile was cruel, cold. "So," he began, his voice lowering to a deadly whisper, "you will be handing over the kingdom... or you will be gone forever."

Inglious and Reid materialized in front of a small, rustic country home. Reid glanced around, confused. "This is my grandfather's house. Why are we here?" he asked.

Inglious gave him a knowing grin, one that made Reid even more uneasy. "You really don't know?" Inglious asked, an eyebrow raised.

"No, I don't," Reid said, his brow furrowed in bewilderment.

Inglious gestured toward the house. "Let's go to the door and see what we'll find."

Reid shrugged and followed, though uncertainty gnawed at him. As they approached, Reid lifted his hand to knock, but the door swung open before he made contact. There stood his grandfather, a wide smile on his face.

"Ah, Reid, you made it! And I see you've brought a large friend with you," his grandfather said, his eyes twinkling.

Reid stared at him, astonished. "How did you—"

Before he could finish, his grandfather interrupted. "Come on in, boy! We've got a lot to discuss. And tell your friend he's welcome too," he added, waving Inglious inside.

Reid followed his grandfather into the cozy home, still grappling with disbelief. "Sit, sit, gentlemen," his grandfather said, bustling around the room. He dragged out a heavy, reinforced chair. "Here, big fella," he said to Inglious. "This chair can hold a thousand pounds. Made it myself... for this very day." His grin widened, a glint of mystery in his eyes.

Reid was still trying to process everything. "Gramps, I don't understand," he finally managed.

His grandfather leaned back, his smile stretching ear to ear. "Ah, child, you forget who we are, our legacy, and the ties we have across the realms," he said. "We come from a long line, with connections and gifts not easily seen or spoken of. We even have seers of our own—not quite like those you're used to, Inglious, but good enough for what we need."

Reid's grandfather's smile faded, replaced by seriousness. "Enough pleasantries. You've come with a purpose, and I have what you seek. As we speak, my sources inform me that Max is already confronting the Koraal Kings."

Shock swept across both Inglious and Reid. They had just missed him.

"Time is of the essence," his grandfather said, reaching to his side and pulling out a gnarled, gray stick about three feet long. He handed it to Reid. The moment Reid grabbed it, the stick dropped to the floor with a heavy thud.

Reid's eyes widened in surprise. "Why is it so heavy? And how did you hold it so easily, Gramps?"

His grandfather chuckled, as did Inglious. "That," Inglious said, bending down to pick up the staff effortlessly, "is part of the magic."

"This will draw those wretched realms into itself. When it's full, it'll try to float away, so hold tight," Reid's grandfather instructed, his voice firm and urgent. He paused, his gaze softening as he looked at his grandson. "Your friend... he's already gone, son. You know that, right?"

Reid bowed his head. "Yeah, I know. But with all our power and knowledge, how come we can't fix it?"

Inglious placed a massive hand on Reid's shoulder, his touch heavy with both strength and sorrow. "Even for the mighty, there seems to be an end," he said. "Some of us may never have to face it, but it lurks out there, inevitable for many. Sure, we could hide away in eternity, but would you really want to spend forever hiding?"

Reid sighed, his shoulders sagging. "That doesn't make me feel any better, Inglious."

"It's not supposed to," Inglious replied, his voice a rumble. "It's to remind you to live while you can." He lifted the gnarled stick, so heavy it pierced the ceiling before he pulled it back down. "Let's go, Reid," he commanded.

Reid's grandfather shooed them off, urgency in his voice. "Go already! Time is short!"

With a nod, Inglious seized Reid by the shoulder, and in a blink, they vanished from the country home.

When they reappeared in the Koraal court yard, the sight was horrific: the ground was strewn with shattered armor and broken bodies. The Kings' armies had been decimated, limbs and weapons scattered like the aftermath of a storm. At the center of the carnage stood Max, his skin an unnatural, charcoal black and his eyes swirling with smoky darkness.

Max turned to face them, a terrible grin stretching across his face. "Ah, you two," he hissed, his voice layered with the echoes of a thousand others. The air thickened as a storm of entities exploded out of Max, rushing toward Inglious like a living flood.

Inglious braced himself, his powerful chest heaving as he let out a roar. From deep within him, another torrent of entities surged forth, crashing into Max's swarm in a maelstrom of violence and chaos. The clash was cataclysmic, a battle of realms that twisted the very air around them.

Inglious hurled the stick at Reid. "You know what to do!" he bellowed, before diving into the fray with Max.

Reid scrambled to catch the stick, but it slipped from his grasp, crashing to the blood-soaked ground. Frustration boiled over. He had had enough. With a roar, Reid transformed into a monstrous, hulking beast, muscles rippling and eyes blazing with newfound fury. But even in his monstrous form, he struggled. He reached for the stick, yet it remained stubbornly immovable, heavy beyond reason.

All around him was chaos—beings he had never imagined shredded each other apart, and the battle between Inglious and Max raged with a fury that defied comprehension. Reid knew he had to lift the stick. Somehow, he had to find the strength.

Reid bent down to pick up the heavy stick, only to find his grandfather suddenly by his side. His grandfather's eyes twinkled with a mix of determination and warmth. "Your friend was right," he said. "I could have lived forever in safety. But taking a risk... well, that's what makes it all worthwhile." With a knowing smile, he hoisted the stick effortlessly above his head. "Keep them off me," he instructed. "Once they understand what's happening, they'll do everything they can to stop it."

Reid swallowed hard, steeling himself. "I've got this," he promised, bracing for the coming onslaught.

As the stick began to absorb the surrounding beings, a shimmering energy pulled them in, like a vortex swallowing the storm. But the momentary advantage didn't last. The creatures caught on fast, and soon they swarmed in, ready to strike. Reid, who had never truly fought before, found himself thrust into a brutal melee. Yet, with desperation fueling his movements, he fought like a force of nature, defending his grandfather fiercely and without mercy. No one would get past him.

Meanwhile, Inglious battled Max with all his might, astonished at the sheer strength and speed his adversary possessed. It seemed that, contrary to what he'd hoped, many of Max's entities still resided within him, lending him unnatural power. Inglious, on the other hand, felt hollow, his own inhabitants long departed to join the fray. Despite this emptiness, he pushed on, unyielding.

Suddenly, Max stepped back from their clash, and with an eerie calm, the entire battlefield fell silent. In that moment, a streak of horror flashed across Inglious's face—Reid's grandfather stood impaled on a dark, crackling sickle conjured by Max, and the battle was staged. The old man's grip on the stick loosened, and it fell to the ground, shattering and releasing the beings it had trapped. Reid rushed to his grandfather's side, but there was nothing he could do. The end had come.

Max loomed over them, his voice echoing through the room. "You have lost, great king of old," he sneered at Inglious. "It was you who decreed us to be bound, and you who chose to become the keeper, hiding away in the shadows to guard what you feared most. How pathetic—a once-mighty king reduced to a prison for his own fears."

Inglious's face twisted with grief and rage. "Max," he spat, "you know nothing of balance or sacrifice."

Max's grin widened, eyes burning with twisted delight. "Balance is for the weak," he mocked. "Look around you, King. Your time is over. This time, you will not return." He raised his arms, and from the sky descended a massive, pulsating sphere, a prison ready to consume.

"Now," Max drawled, "I could ask you to step inside willingly, but we both know that isn't going to happen." With a casual wave of his hand, he commanded the surrounding entities, who surged toward Inglious, their forms twisting and merging to force him into the sphere.

Inglious's voice rang out, desperate and raw. "I thought you had changed!" he roared at the entities that had once called him their vessel.

The masses hissed and cackled, a chorus of malevolent glee. "We do not change," they jeered. "We change things. We are what we are, and we embrace it. Reflection is weakness." Their roar grew deafening as they closed in, crashing against Inglious with relentless fury.

Reid cradled his grandfather's lifeless body, tears streaming down his face. Grief twisted into searing rage, and he turned his glare on Max.

With a roar, he sprang forward, ready to take on the dark force alone. But before he got close, chaos erupted from above: creatures rained down from the sky, and massive ships unleashed hordes of warriors. Portals burst open, scattering waves of powerful beings onto the battlefield. Every force of nature and nightmare seemed to converge, crashing into the swarm surrounding Inglious, and a new, furious battle exploded.

With the sudden reprieve, Inglious finally drew a full breath and locked eyes on Max. Reid, charging through the melee, was quickly swept up in the whirlwind of combat. Before Inglious could advance, the fight reached a fever pitch as two enormous birds made of fire descended, with two even more titanic beings than any colossi. These primal forces tore into Max, ripping him apart. As they did, the entities Max had trapped within himself poured out in waves, the ground began to tremble. Cracks splintered open in the ground, and a colossal soul-eater surged forth, devouring the escaping souls in one mighty, gaping maw. It turned, consuming more and more until it had feasted on every last entity that had dared to escape.

Inglious surveyed the battlefield, awestruck. Creatures from every realm—beasts, hybrids, and even soul-eaters—had appeared, fighting side by side. But just as quickly as they had arrived, they vanished, leaving behind a battlefield littered with silence and dust. Inglious rushed to Reid, meeting him halfway across the courtyard.

Reid's shoulders sagged as he spoke, voice breaking. "My grandfather... he didn't make it."

Inglious's eyes softened, a rare smile touching his lips. "Oh, didn't he?" he said with a hint of mystery. "Turn around, kid. And maybe, just maybe, shift back."

Reid paused, realization dawning. He transformed back into his human form, heart pounding with the spark of hope, and slowly turned around.

"Hey there, boy," Reid's grandfather said, a wide grin spreading across his face. Reid's eyes widened, disbelief rendering him speechless. "But... I saw you—" he stammered.

His grandfather chuckled warmly. "I told you, didn't I? We have our connections."

Before Reid could say more, a magnificent being descended from the sky. Its presence radiated power, and it landed with a grace that made the ground tremble slightly. The figure knelt before Inglious, bowing deeply. "O great King of Old, will you accept the crown once again and rule?" he asked reverently.

Inglious felt a sensation he had long forgotten, something like hope mingled with purpose. He placed a hand on the being's shoulder, his voice resonant with newfound resolve. "Arise, Kaleed. I accept. Let us restore order to all the realms."

And true to his word, Inglious set about mending the fractured kingdoms. He rallied his armies, even welcoming new allies from across the realms, including the once-marginalized hybrids. They were no longer outcasts but celebrated heroes. Word of their bravery spread far and wide, and their strength became a legend.

On the day Inglious was to be reseated upon his throne, the festivities were grand. Reid and his grandfather were honored guests, alongside countless others who had come to witness the momentous occasion. Inglious addressed the gathered multitudes, his voice carrying across the crowd. He recounted the trials they had faced, sparing no praise for the hybrids and their contributions. He even extended his gratitude to the soul-eaters, acknowledging their unexpected role in preserving balance, despite the old pain they had caused by wiping out the Ethric Seers.

As he spoke, a ripple of silence spread through the air, and a figure appeared—a being that seemed to defy time and space, like a spectral echo made manifest. Inglious rubbed his eyes, and in the blink of an instant, the being stood before his throne, halting time itself. The crowd remained frozen, suspended in an eerie stillness.

The being looked like a wretched, spectral man wrapped in decaying, tattered cloth. It raised a skeletal hand, signaling Inglious to approach. Inglious descended the throne's stairs but stopped short when the being lifted its hand, commanding him silently.

No words were exchanged. Instead, it gestured for Inglious to open his hand. Inglious complied, his pulse thudding. The being parted its decrepit mouth, and a harrowing, hollow gasp escaped. From the darkness within, seven glowing orbs of blue light drifted out, shimmering with a strange, ethereal beauty. One by one, they nestled gently into Inglious's open palm.

The decrepit figure gestured for Inglious to open his other hand. With a sense of awe and anticipation, Inglious obeyed, and a final small orb of light drifted into his palm. The creature then lifted its head, locking its hollow, unearthly gaze with Inglious. Though no words passed between them, a deep understanding settled into Inglious's mind. The creature gave a slight, respectful bow before vanishing into the ether, and suddenly, time resumed.

The crowd blinked in confusion, now seeing Inglious standing at the bottom of the throne's stairs, glowing orbs of light resting in his hands. Murmurs of wonder rippled through the gathering.

"The soul eaters have presented us with gifts," Inglious declared. With a fluid motion, he tossed the shimmering orbs into the air. They hung for a heartbeat, suspended like stars, then began to transform, coalescing into familiar forms. Gasps of amazement swept through the crowd as the figures solidified: the seven Ethric Seers, restored in radiant glory, and an eighth figure—Max.

Reid's eyes widened, and he rushed forward. "Max! Is that really you?"

Max's lips curved into a smile. "It is," he said, looking around with confusion. "Where are we?"

Reid laughed, joy breaking through the chaos and grief of the day. "I'll explain everything when we get home."

Max shrugged, still a bit dazed. "Okay. Sounds good."

Inglious resumed his place as king, ruling with wisdom and fairness. He ensured the Ethric Seers, returned by the soul eaters, were restored to their rightful positions, bringing balance and wisdom back to the realms.

Meanwhile, Reid and Max had a long conversation. Reid chose his words carefully, not wanting to reveal too much. Max's last clear memory was being underwater, attacked by something terrible, and Reid figured his friend didn't need to know that he had gone dark and dangerous. So, Reid kept the story simple. He told Max they had been at one of his family's bizarre gatherings, explaining away the strange things around them as part of that. As for the underwater incident, Reid simply said it had left Max a bit foggy, but a good outing had brought him back to himself.

"Right?" Reid asked, hoping to convince him.

Max rubbed his head, a thoughtful look crossing his face. "Yeah, it's all a blur. How did we escape that guy and his goons, anyway?"

"Don't worry about it," Reid said, clapping Max on the back. "Just be glad you're here and not stuck with those people anymore. Alive and free, that's what matters."

Max's eyes brightened with mischief. "You're right. I feel great!" He paused, then turned to Reid with a wicked grin. "Hey, how about we go visit your grandfather? I've never met him, and he sounds... interesting."

Reid's smile faltered, and he shot Max a puzzled look. "What are you talking about? You've met my grandfather at least a hundred times."